Mia

by
Laurence Yep

★ American Girl®

To Cory and Lee Labov, who are stars in their own right

Published by American Girl Publishing, Inc.
Copyright © 2008 by American Girl, LLC

Printed in China
08 09 10 11 12 LEO 10 9 8 7 6 5 4 3 2 1
Illustrations by Robert Papp

Questions or comments? Call 1-800-845-0005, visit our Web site at **americangirl.com**, or write to Customer Service, American Girl, 8400 Fairway Place, Middleton, WI 53562-0497.

Picture credits: p. 124—© Bob Winsett/Corbis; p. 125—© Dann Tardif/Corbis; p. 126—© Lawrence Manning/Corbis; p. 127—© Dann Tardiff/Corbis; p. 128—© Julian Winslow/Corbis; p. 129—© Soren Hald/Getty.

Cataloguing-in-Publication Data available from the Library of Congress.

Contents

1

The Beast and Me

I didn't mean to run over Vanessa with the Beast, and I was really sorry afterwards. Or pretty sorry. Okay, *almost* sorry. But I bet that I'm not the only one from the club who's at least thought about doing it.

That Friday afternoon, the Beast, the Lucerne's old ice-resurfacing machine, had broken down at the worst possible time—right before the arrival of the new head coach. She was coming to be in charge of the Lucerne Skate Club and the whole rink itself. Among other duties, she was taking over the students of the former coach, Mr. Nelson, but we knew that eventually she would select her own group of skaters.

I'd been one of Coach Nelson's skaters, but I had never really understood why he'd bothered with me. All he ever did was point out my mistakes. I fully expected the new head coach to assign me to one of the assistant coaches after she saw me skate.

Bob, the rink superintendent, was working frantically to fix the Beast. He dreams of souping it up and racing it against other ice resurfacers. So far, though, he's had to satisfy himself with painting the

Beast's name in large letters on the side and adding stripes and other detailing.

The problem that day was that the rink was really crowded because a lot of people from the skating club had shown up early and were skating while they waited for the new head coach to arrive.

Normally, I would have hung out with my best friend, Anya Sorokowski, but I was trying to help Bob. It is all my parents can do to pay for my lessons and skate club fees, so, in addition to their volunteer efforts with skate club activities, I help out at the Lucerne in exchange for ice time.

But I can't complain. My three hockey-crazy brothers all work part-time to help pay for *their* skating expenses. Even so, both of my parents are holding down a couple of jobs.

I usually help with all the dull, boring things that need to get done at the rink: emptying trash, putting towels in the locker rooms, sweeping the floors, and so on. But Bob had asked me to sit on the resurfacer and turn it on when he told me to. So there I was, perched on top of the Beast like a sparrow on a boulder, with a good view of the other skaters.

Vanessa Knowles is ten, just like me, but that's about the only thing we have in common. She has long dark hair, bright blue eyes, and flawless skin.

I, on the other hand, have freckles that I once tried to rub out with my eraser without any luck. And when I was small, my coppery red hair and green eyes made me stand out from the other kids. A few of the denser kids even tried to tease me about my hair until I set them straight—you don't grow up with three older hockey-playing brothers without learning how to defend yourself.

I told my mother that we could solve everything if she would just dye my hair blonde, but she said that plenty of distinguished people had red hair, including Mark Twain.

But I'd already looked up some names on the Internet. "So did Genghis Khan," I said to her.

Despite all my tears and pleas, my hair stayed the same color.

It really isn't fair, though. Not only was Vanessa born beautiful, but she can afford the best of everything, from clothes to skates to the recently removed braces that gave her a perfect smile.

Almost always dressed in pink, Queen Vanessa *always* expects everyone to get out of her way when she skates. Even Chad had to twist away from her path— which he did with his typical easy grace. At sixteen, he is a senior-level skater who did well at this year's Sectional competition.

I saw Anya gliding across the ice. Her mother used to skate professionally in Europe, so skating is in Anya's blood. Though we're both ten, Anya is a lot shorter than me. She's as pretty as a doll, with big brown eyes and long blonde hair that she usually ties into a bun for practice.

Anya joined the club two years before I did, so between that and her background, she is a lot better than me. She *should* be a level ahead of me, but she always messes up at the tests or in competitions. However, when she's skating just for fun, like now, she floats along like a leaf in the wind.

Suddenly I heard a bonging as Bob tapped the Beast's side with his wrench to get my attention.

"Earth to Mia, Earth to Mia," he called up to me. "Waken the Beast."

"Sorry," I said. "I didn't mean to daydream."

I turned the key, and the Beast gave a loud cough and sent out a huge puff of black smoke. Beneath me, I felt the machine vibrating and bouncing like an elephant on a trampoline.

"You fixed it!" I congratulated him.

Vanessa skated toward us with both hands on

her hips, glaring up at me. "Now get that monstrosity out of here."

I had started to get off the seat so that Bob could climb up when the Beast began to creep forward. A snail could have outraced us, so I wasn't worried.

"Put the brake back on," Bob shouted.

"But I didn't touch the brake," I said, holding up my hands helplessly. "Where is it?!"

Bob started after me, but he tripped and fell, sprawling on the ice.

"Get out of the way, you dope!" Vanessa yelled, waving her arms like a windmill as the Beast crawled toward her at barely one mile per hour.

Grabbing the wheel, I turned left. Unfortunately, so did Vanessa. I didn't think anyone's eyes really got as big as saucers until I saw hers actually do it.

Suddenly there was a shadowy blur on my right. A woman I'd never seen before jumped up beside me. She had a mop of blonde hair and a large, sharp nose. Grabbing the key, she twisted it, and the Beast died.

We both breathed a sigh of relief. "*That's* what you should have done," she said.

Someone gave a frightened squeak, followed by a *thunk* and then a soft *pflop*. Startled, I looked over the side and saw Vanessa flat on her back, with those still-wide eyes staring up at the ceiling lights.

I covered my mouth with my hands. "I've killed Vanessa."

The woman jumped down and took Vanessa's wrist to feel for a pulse, but Vanessa sat up and jerked her hand away. "What do you think you're doing?" she asked in outrage. Then she noticed me still on top of the Beast. "I'm going to have you arrested," she spat at me.

"No, the resurfacer had already stopped. You were too scared to halt, so it was *you* who ran into it," the woman said firmly, giving Vanessa a quick inspection for sprains or broken bones. "Go ahead and get up, Vanessa. You're fine."

Vanessa spluttered like a pink motorboat engine. "Who are *you?*"

"Emma Schubert," the lady said.

Emma Schubert was the name of the new head coach, Mr. Nelson's replacement.

Bob pulled off his glove and stuck out his hand. Noticing the grease, he tried to clean his palm without much success by wiping it on his pants. Then he extended his hand again. "I'm Bob Gunderson."

Ms. Schubert stood up and shook his hand, dirt and all. "Glad to meet you." Then she looked up at me.

"I'm going to have you arrested," Vanessa spat at me.

"Have you got a name, or are you just part of this machine?"

I clambered down from the seat. "I'm Mia . . . Mia St. Clair."

Her lips moved as she repeated my name silently, filing it away in her mind. "What are you doing up there? Only employees should be using rink equipment."

I was too petrified to say anything, so Bob spoke for me. "She *is* an employee, more or less. Part of the Lucerne family, so to speak."

"I . . . I work here . . . in exchange for ice time, " I stammered. "I take lessons here."

"St. Clair . . . hmm, I don't recall that name." Ms. Schubert took a list from her coat pocket and scanned it quickly. "Well, never mind. Just don't let her up on that thing anymore," Ms. Schubert ordered Bob. "We were lucky this time."

"Yeah, Vanessa might have dented the Beast," Bob joked. Then he swallowed when Ms. Schubert frowned. "Sorry," he said.

She climbed back up onto the Beast and stood there, proud as an eagle, for a moment. When she clapped her hands, the sound echoed like gunshots under the high ceiling of the rink. "Everybody gather around!" she called.

The Beast and Me

Everyone was already watching from a distance, but now all the skaters collected around the commanding figure. "I'm Emma Schubert, the new head coach," she said. She turned slowly as if examining each skater. Not a few looked away from that hawk-like gaze. "I'm going to meet with each of you over the next couple of weeks and assess your strengths and weaknesses. You probably all dream about making Nationals and even the Olympics, and I'm going to try my hardest to see that you do. If you listen to me—and work hard—you'll be ready to match yourselves against the best skaters our sport has to offer. And yet, I'll make each of you into a competitor that, win or lose, people will always point at and say, 'There goes a good sport.'

"But your toughest competition will always be your own selves. You'll want to be stronger, fitter, and better at skating every time you set foot on the ice."

She let that sink in for a moment and then went on. "And even if you never get to stand on a podium, figure skating is a great sport. It teaches you about yourself. You'll find feelings that you never knew you had—and figure skating will let you express them better than any words could. And helping you learn *that* is my real job." She spread her hands in dismissal. "That's all. Thank you."

As the skaters dispersed, she said to Bob, "Please get this piece of junk off the ice somehow before we have another accident." Then she jerked her head at me. "Don't you have something else to do?"

"Yes, ma'am," I said, and was glad to make my escape.

I had certainly started off on the wrong foot with Coach Schubert, so I was glad to get away and do my chores.

2

The Flop Heard Round the World

Between skating and working to pay for it, I spend a *lot* of time at the Lucerne. Bob and his wife, Mona, who also works at the Lucerne, have even set up a corner of the main office so that I can do homework there, squeezed in between skate club practice and my rink chores. Perry, my oldest brother, always asks how I can stand performing such menial tasks at the rink. But Bob says we are really hosts who are just being hospitable to our guests. So as I sweep the floors or change the trash bags, I imagine myself helping Mom clean up our house, and I try to do as good a job as I can.

As I worked, I tried not to think about my next meeting with Coach Schubert and instead concentrated on my usual Friday afternoon routine. It was satisfying to check off each item on my To Do list. Even the old coach, who'd said I had two left feet, had not been able to criticize how hard I worked off the ice. I might be hopeless as a skater, but I am a genius as a janitor.

The assistant coaches who handle a lot of the general classes in skating and ice dancing started to drop by to meet Coach Schubert, so the building was starting to fill up. And, as I've learned, the more people you have, the more garbage you get.

I was just changing the trash bags in the offices when I heard the noise in the boardroom. It's a large room where the club's board of directors meets and where skate club parent volunteers meet and work on costumes and programs and things like that. But most of the time the club's members use it as a social room.

When I peeked inside, I saw a lot of the club's skaters seated on the floor or on the big table that had been pushed against the wall. Vanessa was standing next to the videotape recorder and television.

I could see that she was still seething over the brusque way Coach Schubert had treated her. "What was all that stuff about feeling good? That's loser talk, and *she's* a loser. But we won't have her long." She held up a videotape. "My father got ahold of this tape as ammunition." And she popped it into the machine.

Vanessa's best friend, a girl named Gemma, said, "Too bad he didn't have it *before* the board hired her." She slipped a piece of gum into her mouth and threw the wrapper on the floor.

I made a point of picking it up and putting it into the empty garbage bag I was carrying, but Gemma ignored me as usual. It's at moments like this when I feel a little like Cinderella in her servant years.

"Excuse me," Izumi said. "I thought she was an Olympian." Though she was born in Japan, Izumi's father works for some big global company, so she has lived all around the world. At the moment, her family is renting a house in the town's expensive subdivision, Lakeview Heights. She's a senior-level skater like Chad and the best jumper among the girls.

"Our coach ought to be a winner, not a loser," said Tyler. He hangs around with Chad, maybe hoping that some of Chad's talent will rub off on him. He looked to Chad for confirmation, but Chad just shrugged.

Vanessa fiddled with the fast-forward button, and tiny skaters began dashing madly back and forth across the screen. Suddenly the tape slowed to normal speed and she straightened up.

As music began to play, the name of the piece appeared across the bottom of the screen: *Swan Lake*, by Peter Tchaikovsky.

"Here it is." She held out both hands, palms upward, like a model showing a prize on a game show. "This is 'The Flop Heard Round the World.'"

It took me a moment to recognize the woman who had just rescued me from the Beast because her hairdo belonged to fifteen years ago and she was quite a bit slimmer. But there was no mistaking that nose.

Vanessa grinned. "Here she goes."

Coach Schubert started into an axel jump.

"Up, up . . ." Gemma chanted.

One turn. Two turns. And then she tried for a third, but even I could see she was at the wrong angle and wasn't high enough. I held my breath even though I knew what was going to happen.

"And *splat!*" Vanessa finished.

The coach landed right on her face, her legs and arms sprawling every which way.

Vanessa hit the pause button and turned. "I want someone who can teach me how to win, not lose."

"You might as well watch the rest of it," Coach Schubert said, striding through the doorway. No one had noticed her standing in the hall.

Vanessa stood there, frozen, as though the Beast were bearing down on her again. Coach Schubert ignored her, searching for the play button on the front of the video player and then hitting it.

The music resumed, the notes swelling in a triumphant crescendo—in sharp contrast to the injured skater who was struggling just to get back up. When she lifted her head, I saw the red stripes beneath her nostrils. Her nose was bleeding.

The Flop Heard Round the World

Out of the corner of my eye, I could see the muscles working in the coach's jaw as if she was struggling to keep her face blank. But I could tell the memory was still painful after all these years. A frightened Vanessa slipped around her and escaped out of the room. Gemma slithered silently after her.

I hadn't seen the place clear out so fast since someone set off a stink bomb in the boys' locker room last Halloween.

I wanted to leave with the others, but even though Coach Schubert was The Head Coach, she was still new to the Lucerne, so I felt that she was sort of like a guest and that someone ought to apologize.

But as I stood there, waiting for the scene to end, there was something about the tape that fascinated me. Instead of heading off the ice to get some medical attention, the young Coach Schubert began to skate again, picking up her routine so that it matched the music again. But she was limping now. It was like watching a wounded bird try to fly.

Even when she fell a second time, she got up and continued. I found myself thinking, *Stop. Stop! Get help.* But she kept on, despite the cameras flashing, despite the lenses zooming in relentlessly on her face. It was twisted in such pain. Was it because of her leg, or because she had spoiled her big chance?

I bobbed and weaved, trying to see past the rushing horde. The last Lucerne skaters were leaving the room as the coach stopped the tape and rewound it. By the time she turned around, I was the only one left.

I twisted the garbage bag back and forth in my hands. "I'm . . . sorry."

The coach stared at me. "Don't be. I was the one who chose to try a triple axel." When the tape had rewound, she ejected it.

When I still hadn't moved, the coach glanced at me. "Yes?"

"I thought you were . . . were . . ." I hunted for the right word.

"Clumsy? Stupid?" the coach asked with a twisted smile. "I've been called both those things, and a whole lot worse."

I gulped. "No, *brave*." The words came out of me in a nervous rush. "I would have given up, but you went on skating." I couldn't help adding, "Why?"

The coach stared at me. "I've read your background file. I understand you're a pretty good hockey player. Why did you choose figure skating instead?"

I got scared because I felt as if I was being tested and the wrong answer would flunk me. "I've got three older brothers and they're all crazy about hockey, so I just grew up playing it. It's fun."

"And figure skating isn't?" she asked.

"I'm not very good at it," I confessed.

Coach Schubert cut in sharply, "Coach Nelson wouldn't have kept you as a student if you were that bad."

Privately, I thought it was because he liked to pick on me, but out loud I said, "I never understood that, because all he did was point out my mistakes."

"And yet you kept on with your lessons," she said, studying me. "Why?"

"Because . . ." I hesitated and then the words came out on their own, "even if he never said so, every now and then I knew I had done something right. And when that happened, I felt so good, so light . . . like . . . I was special." I cringed, getting ready for her to laugh at me.

She was nodding her head approvingly. "It'd be easy to choose hockey because it's so familiar, but it won't let you grow as a person as much as figure skating does. Hockey's a great sport, but it sounds as if it doesn't challenge *you* in the same way."

"I guess," I said uncertainly. And I guess that I should have made my own escape then, but I'm stubborn. "But you didn't answer my question."

"You have to earn it first," the coach said. "See you early tomorrow."

3

The Rink Rat

Saturday morning, I woke at 6 A.M., as I always do, to the morning music of our house. In the basement, two floors below, our old furnace was rattling to life, and I could hear Mom in the kitchen grinding coffee beans. I left my pajamas on my bed and reached for the clothes I'd laid out the night before. After I was dressed, I checked myself in the mirror. Thanks to Mom's part-time job at a boutique in town that caters to wealthy college kids, I manage to dress as nicely as anyone else at the rink.

Tiptoeing out of my room, I paused in the hallway to listen to the odd music Dad and my brothers make when they are sleeping. Dad's snores were syncopated by the rumblings of my three brothers. From the boys' room, my brothers sounded as if they were sawing wood at three different pitches.

By the time I walked into the warm kitchen, Mom was sitting at the computer reviewing her skate club newsletter while she sipped her coffee. She's the volunteer editor.

"Good morning, honey," she said with a drowsy

smile. "Did you sleep all right?"

"Okay, except I'm pretty nervous about my first lesson with the new coach," I said, between gulps of the orange juice and toast she'd set out for me.

"Oh, Mia, how can she help but like you?" Mom asked. "You're a strong skater, you're a hard worker, and you don't give up."

I didn't bother to mention that I'd already met Coach Schubert, or what had happened. Instead, I just thanked Mom for her moral support with a kiss and said, "Well, I'd better go. I don't want to be late." I put my plate into the sink and said, "See you tonight."

Mom put down her coffee cup. "I can throw on my coat and run you over quick."

"Thanks, but I'll walk. It's already light out, and there's all that nice new snow."

"Okay, then. Good luck!" called Mom as I left the kitchen.

My skate bag was by the front door, where I'd put it last night, packed and ready to go. I tugged my cap snug over my head, I zipped up my jacket, and around my mouth I wound the scarf Mom had knitted for me last Christmas—there's never much money for Christmas presents, so we usually make all our gifts for one another. It's a St. Clair family tradition.

The Rink Rat

I tried to pull on one of my boots but could only get my foot halfway in. When I stuck my hand into the boot, I found a plug of wadded-up newspaper. It had to be Perry's handiwork. He may be the oldest brother, but he's the biggest jokester in the family.

Once I'd cleared both my boots and pulled them on, I stepped outside and paused in the pale early-morning light. Partly it was the shock of the cold after the warmth of our house. Partly it was to check for patches of ice. But mainly it was just to look around me and enjoy the dawn. Last night's snowfall had transformed houses and bushes into sugar-coated pastries. Beyond the frosted rooftops, the sun was just starting to rise across the frozen lake. Up and down the block, I could hear the sound of snow shovels scraping across concrete. A few houses away the paperboy was struggling through huge snowdrifts. He was one of my brothers' friends, and he called out a greeting to me after he tossed a paper. Then the Matteos gave me a friendly toot as they drove by with their matching snowmobiles on a trailer.

I waved back and went down the steps, listening to the new snow grunt as it compacted beneath my boots. My breath rose in little white ribbons from behind my scarf.

Mia

We live only three blocks from the Lucerne, but the snow was deep and the going was slow because the roots of the trees along the sidewalk have pushed up the slabs into little tilted hills. In winter, melted snow fills the depressions, creating icy patches, and each new snowfall hides them. It's easy to slip and sprain an ankle—and I wasn't going to let that happen before my first lesson with Coach Schubert!

Ahead of me, the rising sun reflected off the Lucerne's big windows so that it seemed to blaze a welcome just for me. The skating rink is all that's left of a large, fancy resort that failed years ago. The Lucerne hotel has long since been torn down and re-placed by houses like ours, but the Lucerne ice rink has remained. The owner built it to look like a Swiss chalet. When I was small, I thought it was wonderful because it seemed like a piece of Europe had been magically transported here. Then I overheard Vanessa, who's actually been to Switzerland, dismiss it as an amusement park fake. I don't care—authentic or not, it's *my* Lucerne.

I rushed through the front door and hurried past the huge cuckoo clock and into the locker room. When I opened my bag to change, I found that Mom had slipped in a sack of cinnamon buns and a note:

The Rink Rat

"Bet you'll be ready for something sweet and sticky after your lesson. Good luck with the new coach. XOX."

I pretended that the buns were still warm, though it would be impossible after the walk through the cold. Mom must have baked them before I got up. She likes doing little things like this so that even when our busy schedules mean we don't see a lot of each other, she can show me that she's still taking care of me.

As I took a small bite, I glanced at my watch and saw that I didn't have a moment to spare. Stuffing the sack and note back into my bag, I changed into my practice clothes, put on my skates and gloves, and went out to the rink.

I feel about ice the way I imagine a sailor feels about the sea. I love looking at the bare white sheet of ice, gleaming and sparkling under the lights. When I first sniff the chill air, my nostrils tingle and I feel alive. Mom says that maybe I'm part polar bear.

Coach Schubert was already out on the rink, wearing a blue fleece jacket and nylon pants. As I did my warm-up exercises, I watched her glide across the ice in a slow, dreamy fashion. She looked relaxed, at ease, especially compared to yesterday.

As the cuckoo sounded, I took the guards from my blades and stepped onto the ice—and left gravity behind. One moment, you're slogging along the floor, feeling as slow and heavy as a turtle, and the next you're gliding, the ice hissing beneath your blades, as if it were lisping out a song.

The coach turned in a lazy arc so that she could skate next to me. In her hand was a clipboard with a thick folder. "I've been reading what Coach Nelson had to say about you, Mia."

My shoulders sagged. "He wrote that much about me?" According to Coach Nelson, I couldn't even lace my boots right, so I was afraid most of the folder was negative.

She slid away. "Let's start with your footwork."

Here it comes, I thought nervously. I could feel my palms sweating and turning instantly clammy in the cold. I'd be lucky if I wasn't busted back to the Twinkles, which is the beginners' class.

I did some basic footwork across the ice, and when the coach didn't make any comment, I started to feel anxious. My old coach had told me only what I *wasn't* doing, never what I *should* do. Did the new coach think I was so hopeless that I wasn't even worth correcting?

She had me do a scratch spin, where I turned rapidly as I stood up straight. As I came out of it, all

she said was, "When you spin, you're leaning too far forward on your left foot, and that's slowing you down. And keep your head up more."

She worked with me on my posture and then had me run through my jumps, giving me advice several times. After consulting the file, she said, "Let's see your double lutz next. Coach Nelson's notes say you're having trouble with it."

Half the time I botched it—which I'm sure he'd recorded faithfully. Feeling as if my doom were chasing me like a rolling boulder, I tried my best but wound up landing on my backside on ice that felt as hard as concrete. I skidded to a stop a few feet away, and she skated over to me. "Want to try again, or do you want to show me your camel spin?"

Her question seemed straightforward enough, but until now she'd never given me a choice. It made me feel as if Coach Schubert was giving me a skating exam—but one whose requirements I didn't know.

If I flubbed the double jump again, the coach might decide she didn't want to waste any more time with me and assign me instead to one of the assistant coaches. And that would mean the humiliation of explaining the demotion to my family.

However, skipping a second attempt would be like running away, so I said, "I'd like to try again."

"Good," she said. She took me through it step by step and then had me do it. When I fell again, she told me as she made a note in my file, "You're taking too long to pull in your arms." She spoke as calmly as if she were telling me how to bake an apple pie. No scolding. No insults.

I tried my double lutz a third time but fell once more. The coach, though, had said that I would be my biggest competition, so I tried five more times, and with each failure I landed on a different part of my body.

Finally, I just lay on the ice, tired and aching. This morning I just couldn't land that double jump.

"Do you want to take a break?" she asked.

Part of me would have loved to rest, but the other part of me wanted to do that double lutz at least once more before I die.

"No," I said, heaving myself up from the ice.

After three more flubs, though, I sat up and slapped the ice in frustration. "Sorry. I don't know what's wrong with me today. I just can't seem to get it right."

"Never apologize for trying," she said. "If it's any consolation, you're already getting better."

"You could have fooled me," I said as I got to my feet, more determined than ever.

I spent the rest of the session trying to land my axel–double toe loop combination and landing hard on the ice each time. I might not ever master that jump combination either, but I was certainly widening my repertoire of falls.

I kept trying, but I botched it again and again. But then, just before the end of the session, things clicked—more or less. I had to put my hand down on the ice to steady myself, but I stayed upright.

I pumped a fist as I glided away.

"Good," she said, making a note in the file. "I was waiting for you to stop a long time ago."

"My brothers called me the human hockey puck when I was small," I explained. "I kept playing them and getting creamed until I could hold my own with a hockey stick."

She smiled. "Well, I didn't expect you to perfect that combination after just one session. What I really wanted to see was if you'd give up. *That* was the real test." She put a hand on my shoulder as we glided toward the opening in the wall. "You asked me a question yesterday and you've earned an answer this morning. I was trying to land a triple axel at the Olympics, which, up until then, no female skater had done in an official competition. My coach didn't want me to do it because I was leading after the short program, but a real champion would rather try to top herself than play it safe. If safety were important to me, I would have become an accountant rather than a skater. Life should be full of challenges."

I was afraid to ask just how big those challenges were going to be. Coach Schubert was nicer than my old coach, but she also expected a lot more, and I didn't know if I was up to it.

"So should I come at the same time Thursday?"

I asked cautiously.

She looked at me, puzzled. "Why wouldn't you?"

I felt relief flood through me. She was going to keep me as a student. "Just curious," I said.

When I was off the ice and had slipped the guards back onto my blades, I saw that the next pupil waiting her turn was Anya.

"How did it go?" she asked. "What's she like?"

"So far so good—" I shrugged cautiously and then crossed my fingers and said, "—I hope!"

4

Challenges

After I changed back into my regular clothes, I started my chores. Saturday is always the busiest day at the rink. Not only are there group lessons, but there're skating sessions open to the public and hockey games— one of my brothers would be playing here today.

I swept the lobby, emptied trash cans, straightened the rental skates on their shelves behind the counter, and then stocked the snack bar with candy bars, bags of nuts, and bottled water. Finally, I'd done everything I could do to get the Lucerne ready for the day's invading horde. Nearly everyone in town owns skates, and almost every weekend they wind up here for a little while. Even though we have a big lake and lots of ponds everywhere, snowy ice is hard to skate on, so indoor rinks are big in this area. Between here and Lake Placid, there are about a million skate clubs.

Anya was still on the ice, though her session was over and the coach had left. The hockey teams had the rink booked next but they weren't here yet.

"Come on," Anya called, beckoning to me.

With a grin, I waved back, went into the locker

room to put on my skates, and then joined her.

She was racing across the rink and, as I watched, she leapt into the air. Landing on one leg, she began to whirl, spine arched backwards as her ponytail swung about like a rippling veil. She looked so elegant that I ached inside because I would never look that nice in a million years.

But I didn't care as I slipped onto the ice, feeling as if I'd gone from caterpillar to butterfly—maybe not one as lovely as Anya, but that didn't matter as long as I could just glide along, no coach, no spectators, just me and my best friend and the ice. Suddenly I saw Anya jump into the air for the sheer joy of it—like a dolphin leaping out of the water.

The sight made me so happy that I rose into the air, too, and even if the landing wasn't as light as Anya's, I didn't care. I was feeling as if I could do anything, so I thought, *Why not try that double lutz that has been giving me so much trouble?* I sped across the ice faster and faster, and then as I began to turn, I extended my right leg behind me, placed my toe pick in the ice, and vaulted up into the air. The double lutz itself was great, but I landed sort of heavily and had to bend my knee too much, so I went crashing onto the ice.

"Try again," Anya urged as she curled past me.

Mia

The coach was right—my biggest competition *was* myself.

Getting up, I carved a curve in the ice, building up speed, and leapt into the air again. This time, everything felt right when I crossed my ankles and clasped my hands against my chest. I was starting to whirl counterclockwise like a top when I saw my middle brother, Skip, in his bright blue-and-red uniform, watching me.

To my brothers, *real* skaters—both boys and girls—play hockey. Figure skaters don't have to worry about hitting other bodies or boards, or dodging sticks, so we rank somewhere below those who do curling.

I was so distracted by Skip that I landed off balance. I brought down my other foot, but it was too late and I went sprawling, body and limbs spreading out like a squished bug.

Oh no, I moaned to myself. *I've just given him the ammo for a month's worth of teasing.*

I always seem to fall whenever any of my brothers is watching me figure skate. I've gone down so often in front of them that I've swept as much ice as the Beast has.

Anya slid over to me quickly. "Are you okay?"

I sat up, wiping ice flakes from my face and

clothes. "At least I've got a matched set of bruises now. I'll get that jump if it kills me." And from all my aches and pains, I thought it just might.

Skip and his hockey teammates were streaming onto the ice. In his goalie's gear, my brother looked twice as wide as he normally does. "That was some fall, Sis," he said as he grinned down at me.

His blond hair was tangled as usual in a rat's nest. He is fourteen, and he's the kind of guy who can comb his hair and have it messed up in five minutes. His real name is René, after one of Dad's favorite hockey players, but my brother prefers his nickname, Skip.

I just gave a grunt and tried to get up, but I was so tired and upset that I fell again—as Skip and his team watched and laughed.

Clacking and clinking, Skip skated over smoothly and held out a hand. "You wouldn't get so many bruises if you wore hockey gear."

I took Anya's hand instead. "Who wants to look like a tank?" I grumbled and got up. But then I added, "Good luck with your game."

"No guts, no glory," Skip said with a shrug. My family says that so often before a game that it has become the family motto—almost like a good-luck charm, in fact.

When I heard his stomach grumble, I shook my

head. "Did you eat anything before you left the house?"

He grinned sheepishly. "Naw, I overslept."

"Mom made something," I said. "I'll get it."

By the time I had changed out of my skates and split my snack with Skip, I was behind in my chores, so I had to double-time it.

When I could, I stopped and loudly encouraged Skip, who squatted in the mouth of the goal. With three noisy boys—four if you include Dad—I've had to learn to bellow or no one would ever hear me.

Quite a few of Skip's schoolmates had come to watch, but they were just sitting on their hands. So, cupping my hands around my mouth like a mega-phone, I let loose a whoop and started cheering Skip's team on. His schoolmates joined in and kept on even when I had to leave to do another chore. Skip's team eventually won, three to nothing, and I like to think I helped Skip a little in beating his opponents.

I was waiting on the rubber mat by the rink so that I could congratulate him when Coach Schubert tapped me on the shoulder. "There you are. Nancy called to say she'll be a little late, so I need you to help out with her Twinkles. She hurt her knee, or something, in all this snow." Nancy is a graduate student at Meredith College north of town, and she teaches the class for beginners, who are mostly five- and six-year-olds. "You can have them do something simple, like reviewing getting to and staying on their feet."

I felt as if someone had just put an icicle down my back. This year, there was a trio of boys—The Three Little Monsters, Nancy called them—who always disrupted the class. I wouldn't blame Nancy if she were just faking an injury and were actually hiding in Brazil.

"I can't," I pleaded desperately. "Can't you just cancel the class?"

The coach handed me my skate guards. "Nancy warned me that there were some problem kids." That was like calling a hurricane a faint breeze. "I could cancel the session, but do you think that's fair to the other students who really want to learn? How would you have felt at their age? Look, Nancy'll be here any minute. Just keep them busy until she can take over."

"When you put it like that . . ." I said helplessly.

"That's the spirit," she nodded approvingly. "Skaters need challenges or they don't learn how to compete." She added mischievously, "Besides, you're bigger than they are."

"But they're nastier pound for pound," I muttered.

5

Three Little Monsters

As if on cue, the doors to the Lucerne opened and parents and children began to filter into the rink. I know this is terrible but I sort of hoped The Three Little Monsters might have caught the flu bug that was going around. But I saw them scamper inside and begin to wrestle one another, knocking over a trash can in the process.

Garbage spilled onto the floor. When their exhausted-looking parents scolded them, the Monsters bent over and started to pick it up. However, it wasn't long before the three boys began to toss the garbage at one another instead of putting it back inside the can.

"A skater can handle every challenge," I reminded myself desperately. "And besides, I'm bigger than they are." But I doubted that this would be an advantage against the terrible threesome.

"Who died, Sis?" Skip asked as he came up the steps toward me, still in his uniform. His hair was stuck to his sweaty forehead and his face was flushed, but he looked happy with the victory.

I looked at his bulky frame. If I couldn't be

armed, maybe I could at least be armored. "Um, Skip, do you have a spare change of clothes with you?" I asked.

"Sure—the team's going out for pizza," Skip said.

"Then lend me your pads and uniform," I said.

He brightened. "So that fall finally knocked some sense into you. You back to hockey?"

Ever since I picked figure skating over hockey, my brothers have been trying to get me to change my mind. "Don't start that again. I just need them, okay?"

"They're pretty smelly," he warned.

"I know that," I snapped as I started to drag him toward the locker rooms. "I could smell you from ten yards away. But desperate times call for desperate measures," I said and pointed to The Three Monsters clambering around the seats as though they were on a jungle gym. Their parents had already sat down elsewhere, too tired to be embarrassed or to try to get them under control. "I have to teach figure skating to that bunch."

Skip let out a whistle. "Maybe you ought to borrow my stick, too."

"I wish I could, but I don't think that's allowed," I said and then grinned. "But after all, 'no guts, no glory.' So, will you help me?"

He gave me a wicked smile. "Anything for my dear, darling baby sister—especially if she'll wash out my gear afterwards."

It was just like the big rat, but I gave in with a sigh. "Do I have a choice?"

While he was in the locker room changing, I sent Mom a quick text message to let her know I'd be home a little late. With everyone going in so many different directions, our family has come to rely heavily on cell phones to stay in touch. Then Skip came out in jeans and a shirt, his jacket over his arm. As usual, he had gotten the buttons wrong.

"Buttons," I said meaningfully, looking at his shirt.

He looked down and shrugged. He started to hand his gear to me but quickly took back the mask. "Oops," he said and rubbed the inside of his mask with his sleeve—but not before I noticed the blood.

"You okay?" I asked.

"It's nothing." He shrugged. "The puck bounced up against my nose, but it didn't get past me. Nothing got past me—it was a shutout!" He handed the mask back to me with a satisfied grin.

Skip's stuff *was* pretty smelly. I promised myself a good, long shower afterwards.

I really looked a sight. Even though I tied the cords as short as I could, the pads hung loose on me and I had to roll up the sleeves and pants of Skip's uniform. I also borrowed a pair of beat-up hockey skates from the rental counter—I wasn't about to use my good blades!

When I came out of the girls' locker room, there was a flash followed by another and another. I put a hand up to shield my eyes. "What're you doing?"

Skip and one of his teammates were shooting my picture with their cell phones and grinning from ear to ear. "I *should* have borrowed your stick," I said, glaring.

"Hold that scowl," Skip said, snapping another picture. It made me think of all the cameras that had flashed when the coach had fallen at the Olympics.

I quickly slapped Skip's mask on my face as I held out my other hand. "Give me those phones!" I started toward Skip and his friend, but there was no way in all that gear that I could catch up with them. Laughing and whooping, they stampeded toward the exit. At the moment, the only difference between them and The Three Monsters was their heights.

The only thing that could have made it worse was what happened next.

"Look at what crawled out of the swamp," Gemma said. "*Phew!* Downwind, girl!"

Vanessa started to laugh and then paused, puzzled. "Who *is* that?"

Glad that I was still wearing the hockey mask, I tried to take the high road and walk by them. However, it's hard to look dignified when you're waddling on skates and legs that goalie pads have turned into an elephant's.

My ears burned as Vanessa and Gemma laughed even louder. Then I heard Gemma say, "Did the coach give you any trouble when you asked for the tape?"

Vanessa said, "No, but she's weird. She told me that she had a better-quality tape, if I wanted it."

I turned and shouted behind me, "That's because she's not ashamed of trying." But they were too busy in their own little world to hear me.

As I walked down the steps, I paused by the mother of one of the Twinkles, who was using her cell phone to send a text message.

"Excuse me," I said. She gave a little jump when she looked at me. "I'm helping out until Nancy gets here. Do you know what they've worked on so far?"

"They've begun to skate short distances and are practicing how to stop," she said.

That was a relief, because that meant that the class had just begun to develop their skills. "Thank you," I said through my mask.

The Twinkles were gathered loosely on the rubber mat by the opening to the rink. They started to point at me and whisper as I approached them.

The first Monster tilted back his head to stare up at me. "Who are you?"

I thought of how Mom handles my brothers and then motioned him over to me. "What's your name?" I asked.

He glanced uncertainly at the others but came forward.

"Jack," the first Monster announced.

I was careful to stand between him and the nearest light so that he was deep within my shadow. "Well, Jack," I said, "I'm Mia. I'm your teacher today until Nancy gets here."

Jack looked me up and down. "Teachers don't wear this stuff."

I leaned forward so that he could see my eyes peering at him through the mask slits. "Well, Jack, *this* teacher does. So let's please get along."

Jack looked behind him toward a man with a neat goatee.

"Dad?" he appealed.

His father laced his hands together and placed them on his lap, a funny expression on his face. "She did say 'please,' Jack."

Taking the guards off my blades, I stepped out onto the ice and skated a few feet away. I risked taking my mask off because I thought I could keep an eye on the Monsters better. "Ms. Nancy is running late," I announced. *Or in Brazil,* I thought to myself. "So I'm helping out until she arrives. As I told Jack, my name is Mia. And today we're going to practice falling and getting up."

I stood by the opening as they all moved onto the ice. I had to steady several of them, letting them pull themselves along the boards until there were a dozen of them in line, clinging to the guardrail.

I pointed to one of Jack's friends. "What's your name?"

His eyes had grown very wide. "J-Jim," he said.

"And you?" I asked his friend.

He slipped behind Jim and peered at me over his friend's shoulder. "Edgar."

"Well, I want you over there," I said, and, taking

Edgar by the hand, I led him to one end of the line and then took Jack to the other, leaving Jim in the center.

Then I had the class warm up by bending their knees several times. Jack was the only one who let go of the boards.

When we had done that for a little bit, I had them sit down and then lean forward on their knees with their hands on the ice. Most of them fell when they tried to stand up from that position, so I kept busy moving back and forth, teaching them how to move their bodies, their hands, and their feet so that they could keep their balance. Jack was the only one who didn't need help, so I'm afraid I didn't pay him any attention.

The next thing I knew, a father was shouting, "Jack, come back here."

I heard the hissing of blades and turned to see Jack wobbling away, arms spread out for balance. "Stay here," I ordered the other Twinkles, looking especially at Jim and Edgar. Then I skated after Jack until I caught up with him.

He glanced at me from the corners of his eyes but went on determinedly.

I wheeled around him in a slow, wide circle. "Let's go back," I coaxed. "Your friends are waiting for you."

"I want to do something new, not this old, boring stuff." However, talking to me had made him lose his concentration and he started to fall. Alarmed, I reached out to catch him, but though he tilted back and forth, he managed to right himself on his own.

He looked scared for a moment, but there was also something in his eyes. I thought it was excitement. Maybe Jack made trouble because he was bored, and Jim and Edgar copied him.

"My coach was just saying that a skater needs challenges or he doesn't develop," I sympathized.

"Can I take lessons from *her?*" he asked. Distracted, he again lost his balance and fell away from my outstretched hand.

He slid a foot across the ice, and I knelt beside him, holding out my hand. "Every skater falls, even Coach Schubert. She'd want you to know how to get up," I said, "because it's going to happen often enough."

If his parents could afford them, some private lessons might qualify him for a more advanced class. I'd suggest that to Nancy.

He struggled to get up without my help but toppled forward. Even so, he didn't quit. I let him try several more times until he was red-faced and puffing.

"I think you're going to make a fine skater someday, Jack. But only if you learn to get to your feet."

"Yeah," Jack sniffed as he lay on his belly.

This time when I stuck out my hands, he took them. As I slowly pulled him back toward the boards, I watched the smile of pleasure spread across his face.

"Every skater has to do the hard, boring stuff before he gets the rewards," I said.

"Yeah?" he asked thoughtfully.

Once we got back to the boards, I invented a game called Sit-Down Tag. You were safe as long as you were standing up, but if you sat down, you could be tagged and become It. And the person who was It could prowl along the line, pouncing on a victim.

I started out by being It but only for a minute. All the Twinkles were a little wobbly and I got Edgar right away. He took short, uncertain steps back and forth once before he caught a little girl called Madison.

By the time Nancy got there, the Twinkles were smiling—and some were even giggling. And they were definitely more at ease on their skates. I'm not sure I raised their skill level any, but at least they weren't bored anymore with getting up and falling down.

As I was putting the guards back on my skate blades, someone cleared his throat behind me, and

Mia

I turned to see Jack's father. With him were Jim's and Edgar's parents. I thought I was going to get scolded for letting Jack wander off and then fall. But instead Jack's father asked, "Um, do you babysit? You get along so well with our children."

"Yes, you have the right attitude and, ah . . . the correct gear for it," Jim's mother added.

They all looked so hopeful, even desperate.

I hated to disappoint them, but I told them I was too busy with my own lessons. I may be crazy, but I'm not *that* crazy.

6

The Riot

It was late afternoon by the time I was done with everything I had to do at the rink. I sent Mom a text message to tell her that I was on the way home. Then I checked my own messages. The most recent one was from Skip, with the results of our *other* brothers' games. Too bad about Rick, who's two years older than me. His team had lost. But the team that Perry, our oldest brother, is captain of had won its game.

As I was getting ready to leave, I saw Coach Schubert fishing her car keys out of her bag.

"Give you a lift, Mia?" she asked.

"Thanks, but it's only three blocks," I said.

"But you're carrying quite a load there," she pointed out.

Well, that was true. And I was tired and bruised, so even if being around the coach made me nervous, not walking home with Skip's smelly hockey gear sounded good.

"I'll call my mom and let her know," I said, waving my phone.

"Good idea. And good job with the Twinkles,

by the way," the coach said. "Several of the parents complimented you. It's nice to know I can count on you to fill in."

Inside I groaned. Maybe there is such a thing as doing *too* good a job.

Outside, cars had filled every available space in the snowy parking lot and Bob was clearing more room with his snowblower, which he loves almost as much as the Beast. Mona knitted him a cap and muffler with teeth to match the Beast's, but the design actually makes him look more like a fireplace elf.

Bob took a hand off the snowblower to wave to us and almost lost control of the powerful machine.

The coach covered her ears at the thunderous racket from Bob's snowblower as it shot cold, white streamers of snow high into the air, like the smoke plumes of rockets.

"Is that a snowblower or are we standing next to a launching pad?" she shouted to me.

"Bob super-powered it himself," I said, pointing to the words "Beast Jr." painted on the side.

"Well, I'm not letting him near my coffee machine," the coach said.

I had expected a big-time Olympic and pro skater to have a fancy car, so I was surprised when the coach opened the door of a battered old Jeep with rust spots and so many dents, I wondered if she drove it in demolition derbies.

She must have seen the confusion in my face because she said, "I bought this with my first earnings on the pro circuit." She patted the fender. "She and I have both gotten a few dings over the years."

As I climbed into the passenger seat I said, "You must've felt good winning those pro contests."

"The scoring is different in those," she said as she started up the engine. "But yes, I'm only human, so I enjoyed beating some of the people that I lost to when we were amateurs. It's a funny thing, though. As many times as I've competed, I still get the jitters before I step onto the ice."

"You mean you *never* get used to it?" I was so horrified that I almost dropped the buckle of my seat belt.

"But I learned a little trick for my nerves," she said, strapping herself in. "I think of a silly jingle."

The coach could be brusque, even tough, so it was nice to see that she had a softer side. "A jingle? And it really works?" I asked.

"Every time." She winked. "I just wish that I'd known that secret *before* the Olympics."

Mia

As she drove, I gave her a quick tour of the neighborhood. Kids were out, floundering in the snow as they threw snowballs. People were clearing their sidewalks and walkways, some with snowblowers, others with shovels. The city's big dump trucks with the plows mounted in front had already cleared the main streets and the crews had scattered salt.

As usual, a store called Nelda's Notions was wrapped in Christmas lights and there were enough inflatable snowmen and snowwomen in the window to start their own village. On the sidewalk, prancing around and handing out bags of cashews to delighted shoppers, was a human-sized squirrel.

"So Zuzu's still around," the coach laughed.

"You know Zuzu?" I asked.

"Nelda's Notions has shops all over western New York, and when I was a kid, it used to sponsor a cartoon show with Zuzu as the host." Lifting her head, the coach began the jingle that went with all of Zuzu's television ads. "'We're just nuts—,'" she began.

"'—about sewing,'" I chimed in. We finished the song together—there really wasn't much of it and it went to the tune of what Dad said was "I'm Just Wild About Harry."

From the way the coach was grinning, I took a

wild guess. "Was that *the* jingle?"

She nodded. "I owe a lot to Zuzu." She added, "And to Nelda's Notions. It had everything I needed for my skating dresses—from special fabrics and doo-dads to patterns. Nelda has even become a friend. When she takes an interest in a skater, as she did with me, she really stands by her. I expect we'll be seeing more of her around the rink."

I was impressed. "You sewed all your own costumes?"

"I couldn't afford to buy them," the coach said. "Don't you sew yours?"

"I'm still learning," I confessed. "I use a dress my cousin handed down to me when she quit skating."

"Well, if you have any questions, ask the folks at Nelda's Notions." The coach nodded her head back toward to the store. "Nelda's got a soft spot for all skaters, and she hires staff who love skating as much as she does. If they don't know the answer, she will. Nelda's such an expert on skating outfits that even professional designers consult her."

The coach listened to the carols ringing through the crisp, cold air from the carillon in the college's clock tower. "I grew up in a town a lot like this," she said. "Enjoy it while you can."

I looked at her in surprise. "I like it, but it can't be anything like the cities you must have seen."

The coach gave me a twisted smile. "I've been all over the world, but I haven't had a real home for a long time. Most of the time I just lived out of a suitcase, whether I was in Atlanta, Grenoble, Paris, or Tokyo."

Our house was the only one that still had snow piled in front of it. My brothers aren't lazy exactly. They'll do chores if someone keeps after them, but they never think of doing them on their own—their brains seem to click into idle as soon as they get home. I love them all, but that part *is* annoying.

When the coach stopped by the snowbank that covered the curb, we could hear hollering from my house. "Is there a cattle stampede inside?" she asked.

I got out and sank up to my knees in snow. "You should see my brothers when there's a pizza delivery at the door!"

"I'm amazed you haven't gotten trampled," the coach said, taking Skip's hockey gear from the backseat.

"So am I," I said. I would have taken the smelly burden alone, but the coach insisted on sharing it.

The Riot

With our arms full, we high-stepped through the snow until I could ring the doorbell. When no one answered—no doubt my family didn't hear me because they were making too much noise—I started to kick at the door.

The coach eyed the old scuff marks on the lower panel. "You've done this before."

"All the time." I shrugged. "We might as well disconnect the bell."

When Rick opened the door, the whooping rolled out like an ocean wave. Although he is only two years older than I am, he is already a head taller. I winced when I saw the hockey pad in his hand. My brothers were no doubt playing a game of tag using a piece of their sweaty gear. Excitedly, he threw the pad back behind him, narrowly missing the ceiling light.

"Hey, Mia! Did you get the message? Perry won! He won! His team is playing for the tournament championship tomorrow!" Rick is always so excited that everything he says comes out a mile a minute and with exclamation points. But all my brothers are just as proud of one another's achievements as they are of their own. Skating for elite hockey teams gives them the chance to compete against the best hockey players around, but they each manage to really stand out.

Mia

Perry appeared at the door, looming above Rick. Last summer, Perry changed from a skinny teenage boy to a gorilla who can out-skate anyone. "And Rick made the winning goal for *his* team," said Perry.

"Yeah, but we lost our other game," Rick said, "so we'll only be playing for third place tomorrow." Rick's team had been at a tournament in a different city.

I started to say something, but Dad rushed out, just as excited as the boys.

"And Skip shut out *his* opponents," Dad said. He was shorter than Perry, but that didn't stop him from putting his arms around his two sons and hugging them. "What a family! What a day!"

As the coach and I set Skip's stuff next to the door on top of someone else's hockey gear, my mother came toward us.

"Mom, Dad, this is Ms. Schubert," I said, "the new head coach at the Lucerne."

Mom said, "It's so nice to finally meet you in person. I was on the hiring committee that recruited you, and we're excited that you're here."

Dad spread his arms in a grand gesture. "Yes, and welcome to the home of the Fighting St. Clairs."

The coach smiled in response. "So it would seem. How do you do? You have quite a daughter.

I can already see that she's a very hard worker!"

"Yes, we're proud of her," Mom said. "Please come in, have a seat."

"No thanks, I have to be going. I'm still getting settled," the coach said and turned to wave to my family. "Nice to meet you all. And congratulations on your games, boys."

Closing the door, I poked Perry and Rick in turn. "That's so great about the goals!" I held up a hand as Skip started to open his mouth to remind me. "And your shutout," I added hastily. "Remember, Skip— I was there cheering you on this morning!"

I really miss seeing my brothers play. Before I got so involved in figure skating, I went to all their games. Their victories were my victories and their defeats my defeats. However, school and figure skating never leave me any time to go with them anymore. I miss cheering them on—and I also just plain miss being with them.

So I made Perry and Rick each give me a blow-by-blow account, acting out each play, and I cheered every goal. And then, even though I had already seen the game, Skip demanded equal time by re-enacting every attempt on goal that he had blocked.

I was just about to tell them about the new coach

when I got distracted by the dirty plates scattered around the living room and the rumblings of my stomach. I sniffed the air and began to salivate. "Did you make pot roast, Mom?"

Mom's pot roasts are the best, the meat tender and tasty, the potatoes and carrots soaked in flavor. I couldn't wait to dig in.

"Yes, but . . . I don't think there's any left." Mom looked distressed. "Your brothers were so hungry after their games . . ."

"You didn't save me *any?*" I asked, disappointed. I don't expect my family to treat me like a queen, but I don't expect them to act as if I don't exist.

"Oh, sweetie, I'm sorry. It was gone before I realized they'd eaten it all. You know how the boys are," Mom said. That's what my parents *always* say whenever my brothers misbehave, and it sort of bugs me. The fact is, my brothers are so good at hockey that it excuses a lot of things they do or don't do.

I nodded. "Yeah, I know. Each one is a vacuum on two legs. But—"

She started to get up. "I'll cook something else for you, sweetie."

I could see how tired she was. Even though she hadn't worked today, I knew she had spent the day

driving from game to game. And the roads had probably been rough from all the snow. And then she made
that pot roast that was now all gone.

"Let me do it," Dad said to Mom. "You take it
easy." He put an arm around my shoulder. "Let's you
and I go scramble some eggs for you."

Perry followed us into the kitchen. "Hey, I
wouldn't mind it if you scrambled some for me, too."

I stared at him, annoyed. "You already stuffed
yourself with dinner." *Including my dinner,* I thought.

He patted a stomach that was as hard as a board.
"I'm a growing boy."

I waited a moment for him to take the eggs from
the refrigerator, but he didn't. *Silly me. Why would he lift a
finger when his little sister can do whatever needs to be done?*

As I opened the refrigerator, Skip popped into
the kitchen. "Make some for me too, Sis?"

When Rick trailed after him, I just raised a
questioning eyebrow.

"Sure, why not!" Rick said as if he were doing
us a favor.

"I actually didn't get much to eat, honey. Why
don't you and Dad throw in some of that good Swiss
cheese, along with an egg or two for me, too," Mom
called from the living room. It is just like my piggy

brothers to eat everything in sight without a second thought.

What is it about boys? I wondered. *How come they can be so clueless?*

As they began to dissect the games again, my brothers kept getting in the way, like large, obnoxious traffic cones. I gave up asking them politely to make room for me. It was faster just to hip them out of the way. It didn't matter that they are so much bigger than I am. As my science teacher says, the correct leverage and the timely application of force will overcome inertia anytime.

After I bumped Rick into the dishwasher, he straightened. "Technique like that is wasted in figure skating!"

"It's been a long time since we had a game on the pond," I said nostalgically.

"Even when you were a shrimp, you wanted to play hockey," Perry reminisced. "You made Dad cut down that old hockey stick just for you."

"You were so cute," Dad agreed, breaking the last of the eggs into the bowl emphatically.

"Until you took that first shot with a puck," Perry said ruefully. "Who'd have thought a twerp like you could hit it so hard?" He rubbed the spot on his forehead where he'd needed three stitches. "Too bad your aim didn't match your strength."

"Who said I was shooting at the goal?" I shrugged. "Maybe I hit what I wanted to."

"Anyway," Rick nodded, "you're a natural."

"You don't belong in figure skating," Skip urged. "You skate better than most of the guys I know, and you handle a stick as well as Perry. You'd be a star player on any girls' hockey team."

"Yeah," Perry said, "why don't you listen to older, wiser heads? You always used to."

I rolled my eyes. They keep coming back to my playing hockey like dogs to an old bone—and right now I felt like the old bone itself.

"I'm not four years old anymore," I pointed out to them.

"Yeah," Rick smirked as he patted me on top of my head, "but you're always going to be younger and smaller than we are. Face it, Sis. Your big brothers know what's best for you!"

"Now, boys, it's Mia's choice," Dad said tactfully.

"But it's the *wrong* one," Rick insisted, and he jutted out his jaw. Like all my brothers, he got that gesture from Dad. All four of them thrust their jaws out in exactly the same way when they're determined about something. When Perry and Skip had thrust out their jaws, too, ready to argue, I got ready for another one of our quarrels. I may not have the chin, but I have the same determination.

Putting his fingers into his mouth, Dad let out a piercing whistle. "Penalty!"

"But—" Perry began to protest.

Dad, though, spread his arms and scooped up all three of my brothers, propelling them toward the door. "Clear the junk off the dining-room table so that we can all sit down together for a change."

I made the mistake of suggesting, "And don't forget the settings!"

"Settings? Well, ain't we gettin' fancy?" Skip called from the other room.

"It's all those fancy figure skaters she hangs around with," Rick said.

Once he was sure that my brothers were clearing the table, Dad came back into the kitchen. "I'll set the table, honey." He grabbed some silverware and started taking dishes from the cupboard.

He looked as tired as Mom. "Let the boys do that," I said and spanked the air with the spatula. "Just give the dishes to them."

Dad returned from the dining room and ran his

hand guiltily through his hair. "I know we depend on you a lot, Mia."

"That's because you're busy working hard for all of us, you and Mom." I smiled. "Now go on, scoot! Out of my way. I'll call you when the eggs are finished."

Grateful for the calm, I concentrated on the scrambled eggs. I'd been wishing I could do something with my family again, so I told myself not to let them pick a fight with me.

Dad came back in to help me carry the platters of steaming scrambled eggs and toast into the dining room. My brothers were standing stiffly at attention behind their chairs. "I forgot the jam and butter," I said.

"I'll get them, dear little sister," Skip said and went into the kitchen.

Perry pulled out the chair where I usually sat. "Take a load off your feet, Sis," he said. He is the prankster, so he was the one who had probably come up with this politeness scheme. He instantly corrected himself. "I mean, please have a seat. You must be tired from all your endeavors."

I wouldn't have expected my brothers to be polite any more than I would have expected a cat to sing an aria. I eyed the pair suspiciously. "Just what are you clowns up to?"

Perry batted his eyelashes in mock surprise. "Why, we're just trying to treat you like the young lady you are now."

"Since hockey's gotten too rough for you, we'll try to act as refined as your friends at the Lucerne," Rick explained with a straight face.

I half-expected Perry to pull the chair out from under me, but he was the perfect gentleman. And for five minutes, my brothers kept up the charade—all the while wolfing down everything on the table.

But my patience wore out when Rick picked up his glass of juice and Perry clicked his tongue. "Manners, old bean, manners."

"How uncouth of me," Rick said. "I beg your pardon." He extended his pinkie finger as if he were sipping tea.

I had already been feeling different enough without them making fun of me.

"Stop it!" Exasperated, I threw a half-eaten piece of toast at Rick's head. He ducked easily from long years of practice.

"Hey, stop it, all of you!" Mom frowned. "You boys leave your sister alone now. And, Mia please eat your food instead of throwing it at your brothers."

But I was fed up with my brothers.

"I'll show you who's gotten soft." I was so annoyed with them that I didn't care if the sock I picked up off the floor was clean or dirty. I could always disinfect my hands after I mopped the floor with my brothers. Rolling the sock up, I tossed it up into the air. "I challenge you all to a game of living-room hockey."

"No guts, no glory!" Perry said and grinned as they all stood up.

7

The Game

It was just like the old days when we couldn't get out to the pond. It was Dad, me, and Perry against Mom, Skip, and Rick. Because Skip wanted to have a turn on the "ice" instead of being confined to a goal, Rick agreed to be the goalie for a change.

The rink is the living-room carpet, and any objects on it—clothes, shoes, furniture, discarded newspapers—are obstacles around or over which we have to play. Our sticks are the empty cardboard tubes from wrapping paper. Hitting anyone with one of them means a time-out in the kitchen, which serves as our penalty box, but there are no other rules.

Laughing, we battled back and forth for a few minutes because, although my brothers may be bigger, I am quicker. Finally, I got the sock-puck away from Skip. Not for long, though, because Mom came up on my blind side and snaked her tube in to steal the puck. Mom had the misfortune to grow up with five brothers, so she learned how to play hockey, too, and can handle a stick as well as any of us.

Dad was our goalie, but Mom faked him out

and sent the sock-puck rolling off our end of the rug.

She gave her victory dance, which involves hopping about and thrusting her tube up like a sword. (Any sportsmanship I possess, I learned from Dad, not Mom.)

Skip and I faced off, so I decided to unleash my secret weapon. If his real hockey opponents knew his weakness, they'd make goals all the time. Skip is as fearless as anyone, but he has a fatal weakness: He likes to laugh.

I started to mug, twisting my mouth and nose and eyes into all kinds of weird positions.

"That's not fair," Skip complained, but he started to laugh like he always does. Not your cute chuckle or polite chortle, but a full-bellied guffaw that ranges up and down.

"Go!" Dad said and threw the puck up in a high arc. It landed between us.

"Make her stop," Skip laughed as he held his ribs, unable to move.

I tapped the puck around some boots and hopped over a hassock, keeping an eye out for Mom. She tried to sneak up on me again but this time I was ready for her, and I slipped around Dad's easy chair so that it blocked her. And then I was clear, streaking toward Rick and the goal.

Rick crouched as he moved to intercept me—and fell right into my trap. With one foot, I kicked at the sports pages, which had been left on the floor near a chair. Pieces of newspaper flew into the air like startled pale bats as I hit the sock-puck at the same time. (I warned you that there are no other rules besides not striking someone with a tube!)

Bewildered, Rick flailed at some basketball player's photo, then at a picture from a volleyball game and the statistics page while I tapped the sock-puck across their end of the carpet. Score: Even.

They countered by rolling up two other socks and then all three coming at us, each with a sock-puck. In the confusion, they managed to knock both the real sock-puck and the pair of counterfeits into our goal. They tried to claim three goals, but we argued them down to one—winning the debate by out-shouting them rather than with logic.

The game went back and forth like that, with neither side asking or giving quarter, and the score remained two to one. From his goal, Rick began a running commentary. If he can't make it as a pro player, he wants to be a hockey announcer.

"And now Mia the Mauler has the puck!" Rick

"And now Mia the Mauler has the puck!" Rick said.

said, pretending breathless excitement. "And here come Skip the Rip and Boom-Boom to take it away." Boom-Boom is the nickname Mom got long ago from my uncles.

I tried to slip around them, but that brought me right along the edge of the sofa just as the sock-puck rolled underneath it.

"Out of bounds!" Skip said.

I got down on my knees and peered under the sofa. "No, it's still on the carpet." I tried to knock the sock-puck back into play with my tube. Mom and Skip knelt and jabbed their tubes beneath the sofa, too.

I finally used my tube like a billiard cue and poked the sock-puck a couple of yards away. We all jumped to our feet and . . . well, I'm a little hazy about what happened after that.

I remember swinging at the sock-puck as Perry and Skip crashed against me from either side. And then I was flying through the air, along with the sock-puck, watching it arc toward their goal while I went over one end of the sofa.

8

Pampered

The next thing I knew I was lying with my legs resting against the sofa's upright back, staring up at the ceiling light through my feet.

"Are you all right?" Mom asked, coming over.

"You boys ought to know better than that," Dad scolded. "Your sister isn't some goon you're playing against. You've got to realize that you're almost full-grown men while she's—"

I think he was going to say that I was still a little girl, and that annoyed me. "I'm fine, Dad," I said, trying to joke. "I'm like mold. There's no getting rid of me." I tried to sit up, but the room started to spin, so I lay back down again. "I mean, I'll be fine just as soon as the carousel stops. Did I make a goal?"

"Game's over," Dad announced. "I'm taking you to the emergency room."

"Don't overreact, Tom," Mom said, but she held her hand in front of my face. "How many fingers do you see, Mia?"

I didn't think twelve was a suitable figure, so I did a rough estimate. "*Unh* . . . three?"

Mia

It was a lucky guess. "Right. But I think you just need to lie down," she said.

My brothers' worried faces loomed over me, big as balloons. "We didn't mean to hurt you, Sis," Skip said.

"Not for the world," Perry added.

They glanced at one another guiltily, as if Dad's lecture was sinking in and they were finally becoming aware of just how much bigger they are than I am.

"I'll carry you up to bed." I felt Dad scoop me up in his arms. I'd grown quite a bit since the last time he'd tried that, and he grunted under my weight but managed to stagger back to his feet.

"Let me do that, Dad," Perry offered.

"Just get out of the way," Dad snapped.

The room had already stopped whirling enough for me to see my brothers standing around, looking shocked at how helpless I was.

I could feel tears of humiliation stinging my eyes. "Put me down, Dad," I said, wriggling in protest. "I can get up there on my own."

Dad tightened his grip. "Don't be in such a hurry to grow up. Let me baby you a little while longer." And he jutted out his caveman jaw.

I realized then that it was useless arguing with

him. And actually, it was kind of nice to get the attention for a change. So I put my arms around his neck as I used to do when I was small and knew that Dad would take care of everything. But about halfway up the stairs he started to slow down, so I said again, "I can manage the rest of the way on my own, Dad."

Dad gave a Neanderthal grunt in response, but then I managed to talk him into just supporting me instead. We went up the other half of the stairway with his arm around my shoulders. Mom was right behind us.

Dad had no sooner settled me on my bed and Mom tucked an extra pillow behind my head than Perry appeared with a bowl of water and a washcloth. He has paws the size of catcher's mitts, but he folded up the washcloth neatly. As he started to lean over me, drops of water fell on my face. "I don't need a nursemaid," I said and started to slap the washcloth away.

Mom put her hand on my shoulder and gave it a squeeze—a silent signal to keep my mouth shut as Perry laid the washcloth gently on my forehead.

Not to be outdone, Skip brought me my stuffed walrus and Rick gathered up an armload of my other stuffed animals and began tucking them around me until my bed resembled Noah's ark.

Mia

My brothers kept fussing over me and generally getting in one another's way. This was worse than having them badger me because, up until now, they had always treated me like one of them. If I got knocked down, they expected me to get up like they would have.

But now after the collision and Dad's lecture, they seemed to have arrived at the opposite conclusion, deciding that since I was too fragile for hockey with them, I was now someone to be pitied rather than mocked.

I was ready to tell them that I wasn't made of glass, but Mom's hand stayed on my shoulder, warning me to suffer their nursing in silence.

It wasn't until my brothers nearly knocked over Mom's sewing machine, which sat on my desk, that Mom finally announced, "All right, boys. Let her rest now."

Dad followed my brothers out but turned in the doorway. "Just give a holler and I'll take you right to the emergency room."

I waited until Mom shut the door behind them and then gave a groan. "If they're like this for a little knock on the head, I'm glad I didn't sprain my ankle."

"They're worried because they love you," Mom said, cleaning my face gently with the washcloth.

"If they really love me, then why do they keep picking on me about hockey?" I groused. "It's not like I'd be in their hockey leagues. We probably wouldn't even have games in the same places."

"But you'd move in the same circles at least. I went through this with my brothers, too. They liked hockey and I liked to dance. They used to tease me to the point of tears." Mom's mouth curled up in a forgiving smile. "But looking back now, I realize they were afraid of losing me. They didn't want to admit that I was growing up to be a young lady with a mind of my own."

"So did you quit hockey?" I asked.

"No, and it's a good thing that I didn't, because that's how I met your father," she said, laughing at the memory. "He was already playing his accordion at postgame parties."

I had to smile as I remembered the family photo album. Dad was usually wearing his accordion in the pictures from that time. But that still didn't help me with my own immediate problem. Even if my brothers could be *so* very exasperating at times, I didn't want to hurt them. "So what should I do?"

"What would you like to do?" Mom put the washcloth back into the bowl. "More importantly, what do you *need* to do?"

I stared at the ceiling for a moment before I finally said, "Even if I did well on a girls' team, everyone would say I learned my skills from my brothers."

Mom nodded. "You'd never escape their shadows, no matter how good you were at hockey."

I saw what she was getting at. "But in figure skating, I've got a chance to make my *own* mark."

"Good," Mom said. "I was hoping you'd say that. You should be competing against other figure skaters, not against your big brothers."

I sat up experimentally and was grateful that the

merry-go-round had finally stopped. "I feel better. But I promised Skip that I'd wash his gear for him. Ugh."

"Don't worry about that now. You need to rest. But how'd he con you into doing that?" Mom asked as she helped me into my pajamas.

So I finally got to tell Mom about the challenges of the day. When I was done, Mom patted my arm. "Well, someone who's done all that *deserves* a rest. I'll get Skip to clean his own stuff."

I fully intended to get up after she left. However, I made the mistake of closing my eyes for a few minutes. The next thing I knew, it was Sunday morning, and when I went downstairs, everybody was in a mad rush to make it to Perry's tournament on time.

"How's the head this morning, Squirt?" Skip asked. He put his arm around my neck in a mock squeeze. "Are you coming to watch Perry play?"

"I can't. I have homework and I told the coach I'd help out at the rink this afternoon," I said. "Now I sort of wish I didn't have to."

Dad said, "Well, you made a commitment, so you have to stick to it. Mom's going to stay home with you today, to keep an eye on you after last night. I wish both of you were both coming with us, though." His big hand gently brushed the hair out of my eyes. "And you're sure your head's okay? That was quite a hit you took."

I nodded to show him my head was working just fine, but he kept on talking.

"Your mom was up checking on you all night," he said. "Why don't you run out to see her? She's outside putting some stuff in the car, and she'll be glad to see you up and about."

"Yeah," I assured him, "I'm fine, Dad. You know me—the human hockey puck!"

When Mom and I came back in, Dad was hoisting Perry's hockey sticks onto his shoulder. "We've got to run. Wish us luck!" he said. He pushed Skip out the door in front of him. "See you tonight!"

Mom and I waved as the door slammed shut. The house grew immediately quiet—too quiet.

I was missing out on all the fun of being with my brothers, but that *was* what I'd chosen, wasn't it?

9

Holidazed

Over the next couple of weeks, Coach Schubert pushed me during my lessons, but she never made me feel bad when I made a mistake—which was often. Still, after working hard, I started landing the double lutz three out of four times. Part of my success was her coaching and part of it was my determination to show my brothers that I had made the right decision.

I was pretty happy with the way things were going until a week or so after Thanksgiving. I'd just finished practice and I was taking off my skates when the coach said to me, "The Winter Show's coming up." Every year, the Lucerne puts on a Winter Show where the best skaters can display their talents and the skating club raises money. "I want you to do a solo," she added.

"What?" If I hadn't been sitting down already, I would have fallen flat on my back.

I'd been in other shows before but always in a pack of skaters where, unless I fell or collided with someone, no one would notice my mistakes. But a solo is the same as being under a microscope.

"We'll keep it short and choreograph it to your skills," the coach said, already planning out my routine, "so it won't be anything too fancy. But I think it's time you start gaining some experience with solos."

"I'm not ready yet," I protested.

"Your old coach seemed to think you were, because it was his recommendation, too," Coach Schubert said. "He said you had real potential."

I thought of that fat folder that Coach Nelson had kept on me. "He did? But he was always . . ." I shrugged.

"Coach Nelson belonged to the old school." Coach Schubert smiled sympathetically. "I had a coach just like him. He loved me like his own daughter, but he would rather have died than tell me that. Spare the rod and spoil the skater."

I felt bad about all the mean things I'd thought about Coach Nelson.

She added, "But he also said you needed to be pushed out of the nest or you'd never learn to try your wings. So guess what?" She put her hand against my back and gave me a little tap. "I'm shoving."

The Lucerne was busier than ever because school had let out for the holidays, which meant more work for everyone. I hurried through my duties so that I could get home early. Before anyone else got home, I wanted to work on my Christmas presents. Last year I had made really simple stuff, but I had much bigger plans for this holiday.

Mom's sewing machine was on my desk, along with the fleecy fabric I'd bought at Nelda's Notions. I used a pattern I'd found online to trace the design for Mom's mittens onto the fabric. But I didn't get any further as my mind drifted and I imagined all the different ways I was going to land on my behind at the Winter Show. Then my brothers would start telling me all over again I ought to stick to hockey because I was so hopeless at figure skating.

I was sitting there picturing all the disasters when someone snapped on the lights. It was Perry. "You know, Edison invented a great gizmo—it's called the electric light."

I shot to my feet. "Don't come in. I'm working on Christmas gifts."

Perry had been observing me closely for weeks, no doubt watching for any signs of possible brain damage from the sock-hockey game. He'd fussed over me worse than Dad. Worried, he leaned over so that we were eye to eye. "Are you feeling dizzy?" he asked.

"Can't I have a moment to think?" I complained. Snatching up the measuring tape, I flicked one end at him. "Scoot."

He paid it no more attention than he would a gnat. "Sure. But first, congratulations on your solo. That's pretty cool, Mia."

"How'd you know?" I asked.

"Annie's mother helps out in the office," Perry said. He's dating Annie, who is also a hockey player. "She saw the list and told Annie."

"It's hard to have a secret in this town," I grumbled.

Perry scratched his head, puzzled. "I thought this is something you wanted. Why so glum?"

"Something always seems to go wrong when I skate in front of people," I said. I tried to be polite by not telling him it was skating in front of the *family* that made me self-destruct.

"You're fine when you play hockey," Perry pointed out. "Maybe you should go back to that. After all, if you don't enjoy figure skating, why do it?"

I didn't have the heart for another argument right then. "Not now, please." I was embarrassed to feel my eyes tearing up.

Perry got that look on his face that he'd worn after our hockey game—like I was a delicate porcelain doll that he'd just dropped. "Sorry, Sis. I mean . . ." He turned and left, mumbling helplessly, "Congratulations anyway, okay? I know we sometimes give you a hard time, but we're all behind you."

I went back to my sewing and started cutting out the fleece for Mom's mittens. When I heard a knock at the door, I hastily covered it up.

"Come in," I said.

When the door opened, Mom stuck her head inside. "It's me, honey. I heard the wonderful news."

"Yeah, isn't it great?" I lied.

Mom knew me too well, though. "Scared? Don't be. You're a fine skater. And even if you make a mistake, it's not the end of the world."

I had my doubts about that. "Maybe, maybe not."

Mom took my hands. "Listen to me, honey. In hockey, someone else gives you the bruises. In figure skating, you give them to yourself."

"I just don't want to let you down," I said, "after all you and Dad have done."

"You could never let us down," Mom insisted. Getting up, she went to the closet and took out my fancy skating dress, which had once belonged to a cousin and had been passed on to me.

Mom held up the green dress with the flowers on the shoulder. "Every time I see you in this, I pinch myself and ask myself if this angel on the ice is my daughter."

"Well, when I put it on, I *do* feel different," I admitted. "Even special."

"You *are* special," Mom said firmly.

But was I special in a good way, or a bad way? We'd all find out soon enough.

10

Rehearsals

We held rehearsals for the Winter Show during the evenings, and despite her promise to keep it simple, the coach had planned an ambitious program for me, with the dreaded axel–toe loop jump right at the start. She said that I might as well handle the hardest part early on, but it made me feel as if I had to scale a fifty-foot wall at the very beginning of an obstacle course.

Even when I landed that combination, I made plenty of other mistakes. Half the time I spent sprawled on the ice and the other half I spent upright, my stomach twisting into knots as I waited for my next error.

Although the stakes were higher, the coach still didn't shout at me when I did something wrong. The only thing she'd say at the time was, "Get up! Keep doing your routine as long as there's music." It wasn't until *The Sleeping Beauty* had stopped that she would advise me about what to do.

"And quit looking like a condemned prisoner waiting to be hanged," she told me.

"There's so *much* to remember," I said in dismay.

The coach nodded. "One of the big Olympic skaters—I forget who—calls it 'herding butterflies.'"

"But why are mine so set on going every which way?" I sighed.

Anya and I always watch each other's rehearsals, and Mom and Dad watch me whenever they are there working with the other parents on the Winter Show. But it surprised me to see Vanessa and Gemma there for my sessions. They smirked and whispered to each other every time I fell.

By the second week, I was feeling like a hamster in a wheel because, besides my regular duties at the Lucerne, I was helping make some of the costumes. I'm afraid, though, that a few were beyond my sewing skills—especially the costume for Rudolph, whose red nose somehow switched places with his right ear. The coach had to have Anya's mom redo it.

The Twinkles' costumes were easier to make because each one consisted of just two big cardboard stars covered in glitter. Cloth straps connected the stars so that they would hang over the shoulders like sandwich boards. Dad and I worked on those while Mom put together the show's program on the computer.

Unfortunately, since the Twinkles were in the background for Vanessa's number, I had to put up with her, too. I kept wondering why her parents weren't there helping out, like the rest of the parents.

One evening as I hurried down the aisle with the newly made Twinkle costumes, Vanessa was getting ready to go out onto the ice. Gemma was there, too.

"Can you believe that coach's pet when she did that sit spin?" Vanessa asked Gemma.

"I thought she was going to drill a hole through the ice," Gemma said.

"And then plug it when she fell into it," Vanessa laughed.

I stopped for a moment because tonight I'd been the only one practicing a sit spin.

"I don't know why the coach picked her for that solo and stuck you with those *babies*," Gemma said.

"My dad's just as mad as I am that I have to skate with those brats, but he says that it's just one more nail in the coach's coffin," Vanessa sniffed. "Because when her pet flops, he'll add it to the list of complaints. It won't be long now before he'll have enough ammunition to shoot her down before the board."

"And then it's bye-bye, loser," Gemma agreed.

I gathered what little was left of my dignity and cleared my throat. Startled, they looked over their shoulders at me. "You can say what you like about me, because I can take it. But don't call the little kids names. Now, may I get by?"

Guiltily, they stepped back to let me pass by with the giant stars.

Jack pointed at my homemade stars and shook his head gravely. "Stars don't look like that. I know. My father teaches astronomy at the college."

I leaned the stars against the rink. "Tell your father I'm sorry, but these are the best we can do."

"Oh, dear," Nancy said, pointing at my hands. "I don't think the glue is dry yet."

When I glanced down at my palms, I saw that they had turned an iridescent silver. "I thought the stars felt a little damp." At least my tights and sweater were clean.

Off to my right, I could hear Vanessa and Gemma doing a poor job of smothering their laughs.

"Why do we have to skate with her?" Edgar asked, nodding toward Vanessa. "She's mean. She called us brats."

I leaned over The Three Monsters menacingly. "Don't!" I said firmly.

Jack batted his eyes innocently. "Don't what?"

"Whatever you're thinking," I whispered. "We can't upset Vanessa any more than she already is. It's not nice, and she can make trouble for all of us."

"If that's what you want, Teach." Jim shrugged.

"We'll have to practice without the costumes tonight." Nancy sighed and signaled to Bob in the sound booth to cue up the music, which consisted of edited clips from Holst's classical piece *The Planets*.

When I got back from washing my hands, Nancy already had the Twinkles and their escorts circling raggedly on the ice. The escorts were from a more advanced class than the Twinkles and they held the hand of a Twinkle on each side. However, skating in formation was new to the escorts as well.

Nancy was trying to get them to leave enough space between one trio and the next so that if someone fell, the following rows still had a chance of avoiding their fallen comrade. The plan was simple: have the Twinkles and their escorts come out, wheel around the rink once, and then stand against the wall, where they could hold on to the railing while Vanessa dazzled the crowd with her own routine.

I went onto the ice to help Nancy, but The Three Little Monsters were actually behaving themselves. Like all the other Twinkles, however, their minds were likely to wander off after a minute, and where their minds went, so did their bodies, so they would tug their escorts off course. This was like trying to herd baby bunnies instead of butterflies.

Unfortunately, Vanessa's patience was only slightly longer than the Twinkles' attention span. As Nancy did her best to coax the Twinkles along, Vanessa stood against the boards, fuming. "I should be starting now," she said, and, staring up at the booth, she drew her hand across her throat several times to cut the music. When the notes died, she put her hands on her hips and turned to Nancy. "*Why* do I have to skate with them?" she demanded.

"Vanessa, not everything is going to go right when you skate," the coach called down from a top row, where she had been watching. "Besides, this is part of the choreography. You can't be the queen of the galaxy if you're the lone star."

I was watching the boys and skated over to Jack to wag a still-silver finger at him. "Don't," I repeated.

"No worries, Teach." Jack grinned. "We're going to be her best buddies."

That sounded ominous. With The Three Monsters as friends, who needed enemies? But I could hardly scold him for being nice to her.

Somehow we got through the rest of rehearsal. Coach Schubert was as good at choreography as she was at teaching, so she had planned a good routine for Vanessa. Technically, I think Vanessa is almost as good as Anya, but whenever she falls, she insists on beginning all over. I don't think I had seen her complete her routine yet.

When the rehearsal was finally over, Vanessa made a point of getting off the ice ahead of her co-stars and, in the process of shepherding the Twinkles off the ice safely, I lost track of The Three Monsters.

The next thing I knew, they had surrounded Vanessa and Gemma. "You were wonderful," Jack said, slapping Vanessa heartily on the back.

"You, too," Edgar said, patting Gemma.

Vanessa and Gemma regarded them with as much enthusiasm as they would have shown to purple slugs crawling up their legs.

Jim went so far as to grab Vanessa's hand and pump it enthusiastically. "I can't wait to skate with you."

"Thank—" Vanessa started to choke out when her eyes shot up in horror and she looked down at her hand, which was now silver. "You little brat!"

Too late, I saw that there were small handprints all over the still-damp stars. The Three Monsters must have coated their hands before they attacked Vanessa and Gemma with friendship.

I rushed over to pull the Monsters beyond Vanessa's reach. "It'll wash off."

"Vanessa, your jacket!" Gemma said and pointed at the marks on her back.

"And yours," Vanessa said to Gemma.

Their jackets were goose down, which you can't wash so easily.

"We'll pay for the dry cleaning," Jack's father said, coming over and sizing up the situation. I wondered how often he'd had to say *that*.

Vanessa ignored him as she yelled at Nancy. "I want these . . . these *troublemakers* out of the routine!"

"No, we need them. They're the steadiest skaters in the Twinkles," the coach said as she came down the stairs with her clipboard, which seemed permanently fused to her hand nowadays. "They'll be dealt with in another way."

Vanessa stormed past the coach with Gemma trailing after her. I was sure their parents would hear an earful tonight.

The coach handled The Three Criminals, all of whom were looking very sorry now that they had attracted her attention, and then gave her notes to Nancy. By then, Chad had taken to the ice.

As the coach watched him intently, I tried to

speak, but it took a couple of minutes to find my voice. "Coach," I said.

The coach didn't look at me but kept her eyes on Chad. "Talk louder. I can't hear you over the music."

"Maybe you should let me switch with Vanessa," I suggested. Her routine is actually simpler than mine, so it would be more manageable for me. "She'd be happier by herself."

Coach Schubert hugged her clipboard. "I assigned those slots to you and Vanessa in the hopes that they would correct both your flaws: she has too much confidence and no persistence while you have plenty of persistence and no confidence."

"But when Vanessa's not happy, no one is," I said. "And . . . and her father's on the board."

The coach arched an eyebrow. "Don't you think you can do your routine?" she demanded.

"I guess so . . . at least I *hope* so," I gulped.

"Then I'll make a deal with you," she said calmly enough. "You leave the backbiters to me and I'll leave the skating to you."

11

Christmas

After that conversation, I was more determined than ever to do well, so, although Christmas is my favorite holiday and I love all the preparations for it, I practiced every moment I could. I'd read about a skater who learned his routine so well that he could do it in his sleep, and he wound up winning a silver at the Olympics.

So when I was home and it was dark outside, I rehearsed constantly in the basement even though I had to dodge around my brothers' drying hockey gear. Or if I was home during daylight, I went out to the cleared pond behind our house to do my routine on real ice. Even at night, I couldn't escape skating because I was having nightmares in which I kept falling during the Winter Show.

But I wouldn't let myself quit. Like the coach had said, each time I did my routine, I was competing against myself. I was determined to do it perfectly.

Then, one morning, I woke up in a panic because it was already daylight outside. I must not have set my alarm, and I was late for lessons! Jumping out of bed,

Christmas

I started to reach for my clothes. Our old furnace was coughing and rattling worse than ever, but above the noise, I heard my family laughing downstairs. Then I remembered—it was Christmas!

From downstairs I heard Dad playing Christmas music on his accordion—except he also slipped in his favorite tune, "Lady of Spain." I smiled as I remembered what it was like to sit on Dad's lap when I was small, sandwiched between him and his accordion as he taught me how to play "Lady of Spain." That song always made me feel safe and cozy. Listening, I found my fingers moving as if they were playing the keys. I guess some memories bring back images, others sounds, and still others are felt in your body.

I pulled on my robe over my pajamas and went downstairs. My whole family was there, my parents sitting on the sofa sipping coffee and munching on Mom's famous cinnamon buns, while my brothers paced impatiently.

Skip snorted when he saw me. "I was just about to go up and make sure you were still breathing!"

As Skip steered me toward the lit tree, my whole family grinned like cats that had eaten a flock of canaries.

Reaching under the tree's lower branches, Skip

held up a small package wrapped in cheery red-and-gold paper. "We can't bodycheck the figure-skating judges for you, so we thought this would be the next best thing to give you," he said. "We all chipped in."

It was too small for a scarf, and when I unwrapped it, I saw that it was a portable music player.

I couldn't believe it! I was on Cloud Nine—until guilt brought me back down to earth. "But—but it's so *expensive*," I said. "And it's not homemade!"

"We all agreed that you could really use it," Dad said. "We made an exception to our tradition this year."

My three huge brothers gathered around me so that I felt as if I were surrounded by tall forest trees. They were eager to explain the features but Rick, the electronics whiz in the family, looked as if he was going to explode, so I asked him to do it.

Bob had burned my music from *The Sleeping Beauty* onto a CD, and Rick had already transferred the music from the CD onto my player. Slipping the buds into my ears, I listened to the first notes of the piece. "It's so clear," I said. "Thank you—all of you!"

After that, the family turned to the rest of the presents, and soon the wrapping paper was flying in a rainbow blizzard. Perry held up the cap I had given him, which was in his team's colors. "Are you trying to tell me something, Sis?"

Somehow the top had come out like a cone rather than a dome, so it looked more like a dunce cap. "It was the first time I tried that pattern," I explained, blushing.

"You've had a lot on your mind," Perry said with a grin as he pulled the cap on anyway.

Rick was pleased with the computer wrist rest I had made because it matched his team colors of green and gold. Skip liked his blue-and-red bike pouch, and Mom cooed over her warm fleece mittens.

But I could see that the seams were so crooked, they pulled each item slightly out of shape. "I guess I should've tried to sew simpler things," I said as my face turned red. "I'll get better by next Christmas."

"But they're all . . . so *unique*," Dad said as he slid his eyeglass case into his new pouch with the bottom that stuck out at a right angle.

"Yes, *unique*," Mom chimed in, and my brothers kindly agreed.

By the afternoon, worn out by the long hours around the tree and a big meal of turkey with all the trimmings and Mom's rhubarb pie, my family had vegged out and sat watching a football game on TV.

I love being with my family and snuggling in

between my parents on the sofa, all toasty and warm. Yet as happy as I was, I felt as if I needed one more thing to make this day perfect, and that was the ice.

So, slipping back up to my room, I changed into my practice pants and a sweater. By the time I put my cap on and walked back downstairs, I was feeling as hot as a furnace.

With my skates over my shoulder, I crept out of the house, walking along the familiar path through the bare shrubs and trees until I reached the pond. I changed into my skates and I stuck my music player onto my waistband.

Yesterday had been warm and sunny enough for the ice to melt slightly, but then the temperature had dropped dramatically. The ice had refrozen overnight so that now there wasn't a mark on it—it was as if Bob had resurfaced it with the Beast just for me. The pond was a smooth white sheet, tinted with lavender and blue, and it made me feel as excited as a five-year-old with a clean sheet of paper to paint on. As soon as I glided onto the ice, the breeze touched my face like cold, silken feathers, brushing away the bad rehearsals, Vanessa's backbiting, and all my other worries, as if they were mere cobwebs.

With the player's buds in my ears, I began my

The breeze touched my face like cold, silken feathers.

routine. As the music flowed into and around me,
I began to skate. It was just me and *The Sleeping Beauty*.
I glided, I twirled, and I leapt into the air joyfully. I was
finally starting to get things right!

But during my fifth try, as I spun in a spiral and
the trees whirled around me, I glimpsed Perry's bright
red cap headed my way. He hadn't taken it off the
whole day.

His hands stuffed into the pockets of his new
letter jacket, he stood on the side of the pond and
watched me. I could imagine all the jokes he was getting ready to make. That was enough of a distraction
to send me spinning out of control like a propeller that
had fallen off an airplane. I landed hard and skidded
round and round in circles across the surface, until I
came up against a snowbank, one earbud popping out
of my ear.

I heard Perry running toward me. "You okay,
Sis?" he asked, holding out a hand.

I took it and let him pull me upright. "Yeah,"
I said a little breathlessly. I thought I'd beat my brother
to the first jab. "I think I've got a future as a carousel
horse."

"Well, you're good at spinning around in circles."
He grinned and straightened my cap. "I knew I'd find

you down here. Mom wants you to come back inside."

"Not until I finish. Coach said to keep skating until you complete your routine." Putting the buds back into my ears, I tried to pick up that point in my routine that matched the music.

I was hoping Perry would go away, but brushing the snow from a fallen log, he sat down to wait for me. I didn't know how to ask him to leave, so I just went on, missing another part that I had done so easily just before. And then another mistake and still another. From the corner of my eye, I could see Perry shaking his head as if he felt sorry for me. He didn't say it out loud but I knew what he was thinking: *You gave up hockey for this?*

He sat there, looking colder and sadder by the second but clearly wanting to keep me company in my misery. And that hurt worse than a truckload of insults.

As I kept on making errors, I felt more and more frustrated with myself. It was almost a relief when I heard the last note and could turn off the player. "Okay, let's go home."

He rose, stiff from the cold. "Your coach actually thinks you're ready for a solo?"

I felt my face turn red as I sat down on the log to take off my skates. "Not all my practices are this bad."

Mia

His hands were still in his jacket pockets, so his arms were bent like wings. He flapped them now. "You can't get out of it, then?"

"No," I said firmly as I took off my skates. "The coach won't let me, and I don't want to. I'm a figure skater. This is what I want to try to do."

"But—" he began.

"It's my first solo." I slipped on my boots, stamping my feet against the ground so that they would go all the way in. "I can do it. I *know* I can."

As soon as I got up, snow from an overhanging tree branch fell onto me. Before I could brush it off, Perry began doing it for me.

"I'll take care of this myself," I said, backing away resentfully.

"Let me do this much for you," Perry said.

So I stood patiently as he flicked away the last snowflakes. "Thanks. It's nice to know I've got a big brother trying to look out for me."

"But you won't listen to him," he sighed helplessly.

I poked him. "I have to make my own mistakes."

"I just want you to know that I'll always be there for you," he said, slinging his arm around my shoulders. As we trudged home, he kept giving me encouraging little pats on my back.

But his pity was worse than any teasing, and it shook my confidence more than ever.

All the way back, I kept wondering if he was right after all. Was I going to stink up the Winter Show? Should I quit for the coach's sake, if not for my own?

12

Star Power

The night of the show, we hung curtains across the doorway that Bob uses to bring the Beast in and out. As a door frame, some of the parents had put up huge cardboard trees, frosted them with white glitter, and hung twinkling lights in the branches. I was assigned to help Anya's mother, who had volunteered to be the show's stage manager.

After some brief remarks by the coach, Anya was to start off the show, but she had to wait for Bob to finish his introduction.

Besides racing the Beast, Bob's other ambition is to be an announcer at wrestling matches, and so his deep voice boomed over the loudspeakers, "And here she is, that Angel of Mercy, that Diva of Delight, that Beauty on Blades. She slices, she dices—An-n-ya Sor-r-r-o-kow-s-s-s-kiii!" he said, rolling her name out as if it had ten syllables.

Mrs. Sorokowski rolled her eyes. "That man!" Her hands twisted her side of the curtain as if she was wishing it were Bob's neck.

Anya just grinned at me as I stood by the other

side of the curtain. Then, taking a deep breath, she started forward. Mrs. Sorokowski and I jerked the curtains open simultaneously so that Anya could make her grand entrance onto the rink.

We quickly closed the curtains behind Anya and Mrs. Sorokowski told the next act—a group of boys dressed as pirates, complete with big cardboard swords—to get ready to go out. Then we both peeked at the rink to watch Anya skate.

Besides being a fund-raiser for the club, the Winter Show is a regular social event for the town, so the seats were packed. However, I can't say that many were paying attention to the actual show. Everywhere, knots of people were catching up on gossip rather than watching the ice itself. And the stairs were filled with a steady stream of townsfolk heading to and from the restrooms or the snack bar.

All that murmuring and movement didn't distract Anya at all. As long as it isn't a competition, Anya is fine. She just seemed to float across the ice, light as a snowflake, to the haunting notes of Faure's *Pavane*. I got goose bumps just watching her.

As Anya came off, looking tired but happy, Mrs. Sorokowski used one hand to drape a towel around her daughter's neck while her other hand pointed imperiously to the waiting skull-and-crossbones crew. "Go, go!" she commanded.

I gave Anya a quick thumbs-up to let her know how great she'd been.

While Bob thundered on about blood, bones, and buccaneers, the pirates launched themselves onto the ice with wicked grins and fire glinting in their eyes. I knew from the practices that their sword fights would be athletic and energetic rather than artistic—and that all the male audience members under eighty would probably eat it up.

Shutting the curtains on the "Carnage on Ice," Mrs. Sorokowski jerked her head at Nancy and me. "Star Power routine next!" she called. "Get ready."

I helped Nancy herd the Twinkles and their escorts more or less into a column of threes to the left of the doorway. They were dressed in black turtlenecks and tights and had their cardboard stars slung in front and back. I had made sure that the glue was good and dry on this batch.

Unfortunately, the Twinkles were also sporting headbands with antennae made from springs tipped with silver-painted balls. The balls bobbed and jiggled, and as the boy Twinkles got more and more excited, they dueled by bending their heads like bulls and then fencing with the ball-tips. It kept Nancy and me busy just trying to keep them from poking out an eye.

At the head of the column, though, I could see Jack struggling not to join in.

I put a hand on his shoulder. "Coach is counting on you, Jack."

"I know," he said, looking very earnest.

Wanting to keep away from The Three Little Monsters, Vanessa was standing on the right side of the doorway, but that put her directly in the path of the exiting pirates, who came off the ice to loud applause, their cardboard swords bent but each pirate grinning from ear to ear. Vanessa barely managed to skip to the side as the cutthroats roared past her. "Watch it," she said crankily, "or you'll tear my dress."

She'd had a new professional skating dress company make her a dress from her own design, and it was so elaborate that she had only gotten her outfit a couple of hours before the show. This was her first time wearing it.

Large gold stars shone on the front, shoulders, and back, and every square inch of her costume was covered with beads and sequins, even the long, wing-like sleeves. She'd also dusted her hair and face lightly with glitter so that she sparkled from head to toe.

Mia

Whenever she stood still, she looked like a giant hood ornament.

As Bob neared the end of his introduction, Mrs. Sorokowski pointed at the rink. "Star Power, go, go!"

A shortened version of Holst's "Jupiter" began to play through the rink. Crossing our fingers, Nancy and I began to send the Twinkles and their escorts out. Jack was in the first trio, holding on to the left hand of his escort, an eight-year-old girl named Ashton. A girl Twinkle, Madison, gripped Ashton's right hand.

As they emerged onto the ice, they looked so cute that *oh*s and *ah*s came from the audience. Madison and Ashton ate it up, but Jack just looked dead serious. Unfortunately, the spectators started to clap their approval, and the applause startled Madison, who tripped. She would have fallen if Ashton hadn't paused and held her up by her arm. I gasped as the next rank of Twinkles closed on them, afraid a collision would set off a massive pileup. But Jack stuck up his free hand. "Halt!" he shouted to the others over the music.

And rank after rank stopped. When Madison had regained her balance, Jack motioned the Twinkles forward. Nancy and I watched nervously as Jack picked up the pace, tugging Ashton along as he skated in short, steady strokes. He led the column of Twinkles and escorts in a ragged arc around the rink, like a snake with star-shaped scales that lurched, slowed, and then plunged forward again.

"Way to go, Jack," I murmured.

Nancy put her hand on her cheek. "But why is he wearing black circles?" she asked me.

I squinted at the cardboard cutouts slung in front and in back of Jack. Instead of stars, they were the shape and color of giant burnt pizzas, so he looked like an eight ball with legs. He must have exchanged them for his star costume when my back was turned.
"I have no idea," I sighed, "but they'd better not be part of a prank!"

I kept waiting for Jack to pull whatever stunt he had planned, but he played it honest as they finally headed for the wall.

"Big Star, go!" Mrs. Sorokowski gestured to Vanessa.

But Vanessa had already tossed her head back and spread her arms. Her smile clicking mechanically into place, she glided onto the ice, her sleeves fluttering like clouds of stardust. There was mild applause from the part of the stands where Vanessa's friends and family must have been seated. As she headed toward the middle of the ice, the Twinkles and their escorts formed a line against one wall, just as they were supposed to.

I was busy helping Anya and Mrs. Sorokowski arrange the synchronized skating team which was to go on next. All the skaters looked very stylish in black skirts, white shirts, black bow ties, and top hats.

But then Nancy called from the doorway. "Oh, no! Vanessa's beads must be coming off."

We went back to the doorway to peer out from behind the curtains. The ice always sparkles a little in the light, but Vanessa was leaving a shimmering trail of gold flecks behind her.

The beads were so tiny that you would probably not even notice if you stepped on them on a sidewalk, but beads are another matter on ice. There's only a thin pair of blades supporting a skater, so it doesn't take much friction to throw off a skater's balance.

Nancy and Mrs. Sorokowski began to wave a frantic warning, but it was too late.

As Vanessa was doing some nifty footwork, she returned to the middle of the ice where she had already skated. Suddenly, she pitched forward, then went down.

"Get up, get up," I urged softly.

As Holst's *Planets* orbited on relentlessly, Vanessa rolled over and sat up, stunned.

"Get up, get up," I repeated.

Finally she got to her feet, but instead of trying to continue her routine, she tried to head off the ice—and stumbled and fell again. I'm not sure if it was more patches of beads or just the loss of confidence, but she tripped a couple more times and finally she started to crawl.

Suddenly I realized that we couldn't let the Twinkles and their escorts head back through that minefield of beads.

I found Jack's silver stars where he had ditched them behind a table and slipped them over my head so that the straps rested on my shoulders with one star dangling in front of me and another in back.

Nancy had immediately figured out my plan and held the curtains open for me as I burst onto the ice. Vanessa lifted her head to stare at me. I saw the tears coming from her eyes. No matter what she was trying to do to the coach, I would never have wished this on her.

"Keep going," I said in a low voice to her. "I'll handle this."

Fortunately, Vanessa had only gone near the wall in a couple of spots, so I kept near the railing, making sure to take small steps through the beaded areas until

Mia

I got to Jack. He was looking stunned and uncomfort-
able, while the escorts and the other Twinkles looked
ready to panic and bolt individually toward backstage—
and create a group catastrophe as they tried to get
through the beads.

"Follow me," I said to Ashton, "and be sure to
keep to the wall."

I supervised the retreat of the Twinkles and their
escorts, taking care to stand by the danger spots until
they had all passed. I didn't breathe a sigh of relief
until I got them backstage without a fall.

Bob had figured out the problem, and after telling
the audience there would be an unofficial intermission,
he put on some music and left the tech booth to come
down to us. As he went out on the ice on the Beast,
I went over to Jack.

"Way to keep your head," I said and then tapped
the black circle in front. "But what's this?"

"I'm a Black Hole," Jack intoned. "It sucks all the
matter into it, even other stars. That's why everyone
else had to follow me."

"I guess they did!" I laughed and gave him a
hug, not caring if I crushed his costume.

Nancy took over from there, taking the flushed,
excited Twinkles back to their parents. Before he left,

Jack called to me, "Break a leg, Teach."

"I'll try," I said, waving my hand.

The synchronized skating team was warming up again as the skaters waited in a column of twos. When some of them shifted, I saw Vanessa through the gap.

She was sitting on a chair, miserably wiping her eyes with one of her now-bare sleeves.

I found a box of tissues and brought it over to her. "Are you all right?" I asked.

"What do you think?" She sniffled as she yanked out a couple of tissues. "How'll I ever live this down?"

"The coach did," I said softly.

She lifted her head and I caught a glimmer of understanding in her eyes. "And that didn't stop her," she said thoughtfully.

"Falls are always part of the risk," I said and then repeated our family motto. "But hey, no guts, no glory."

"Yeah." She nodded her agreement. "No guts, no glory." She actually smiled at me for the first time that I could remember. "Good luck out there, Mia."

13

The Toughest Two Minutes

When Bob had finished clearing the ice and had returned to the booth, the show began again. After the act before mine went on, I listened to my player as I started to warm up. All too soon, Anya was signaling me that it was time.

As I handed my player to her, Mrs. Sorokowski handed me a note. "The coach said to give this to you before you went on."

I unfolded the paper and read, *Coach Nelson believed in you and so do I. Now all you have to do is believe in yourself.*

As the skaters in padded snowman costumes were bobbing offstage past me, Bob was beginning his introduction for me. "And here she is, that Dynamo of Demolition." He was pulling out all the stops for me. "That Miss of Mayhem, that Classy Lassie, that . . ."

Nervously I adjusted the strap of my dress. *You did this perfectly during practice,* I told myself. *You can do it now.*

"Mia, good luck!" Anya said.

As I slipped through the doorway, I kept telling

myself that this was just like practice. But that was a lie because I'd never had so many people watching me alone on the ice. So many people, plus my family. The odd thing, though, was that the stairs were clear, as if everyone had actually stopped to see me. And I was sure that half of them had camcorders or cell phones that took pictures, so my catastrophe was going to be well recorded.

Well, no guts, no glory, I reminded myself silently. But as I headed for the center of the ice, I could feel my body tensing from the bottom of my toes to the tips of my hair until I felt like one big, giant coiled spring.

Through the window of the tech booth, Bob gave me a thumbs-up. "NOW, BRING YOUR HANDS TO-GETHER FOR M-M-M-I-I-I-A S-S-S-S-A-I-N-T-T-T C-C-C-L-L-A-I-R-R-R!" he boomed.

Loud clapping broke out from where my family was seated. Jack and the other Monsters were almost as boisterous in another part of the seats. "You show 'em, Teach!" Jack shouted.

Despite my nerves, I couldn't help smiling as I heard his parents busily shushing him. But not to be outdone, Skip let out one of his piercing whistles, and I was so surprised that I tripped. Arms flailing, I stumbled forward.

Mia

Pure instinct brought my arms up, and I began to flail them. It wasn't exactly the graceful entrance I'd hoped for. A few people laughed nervously, but I managed to regain my balance.

Cheeks burning, I went to my starting spot and struck my pose. I hadn't expected the catastrophe to begin before the routine itself! My poor parents. They had made so many sacrifices for my dreams. And how did I reward them? With this fiasco. My brothers were right. What had *ever* made me think I could be a figure skater? In a moment, I'd make my whole family into laughingstocks.

The frightened, guilty thoughts whirled round and round inside my head, driving out everything else. Suddenly I couldn't remember my first step. Or the next. My mind was a complete blank. I could feel the panic rising inside me. I wished Bob would start up his introduction again and go on, oh, for maybe an hour.

What was worse than Vanessa having to crawl over the ice? Me, with my legs turning to icicles, stuck in the middle of the rink. Mrs. Sorokowski was going to have to get the pirates to carry me off the ice.

Only a few seconds passed, but it felt like a lifetime as I stood there wishing the pirates would fetch me. I was so scared about the coming disgrace that

I started to tremble and my fingertips began to twitch.

I just wanted to get off the ice, away from the staring eyes and the smirking faces. Then I'd find some dark place where no one would ever see me—some spot where I could huddle, somewhere safe.

Safe.

It took me a moment before I realized that my fingers were moving in a purposeful way on their own. And it was another second before I understood that they were trying to play "Lady of Spain" on the accordion.

And suddenly I remembered, as vividly as if it were happening right now, sitting on Dad's lap with his accordion pressed up tight against me. I could barely reach around it to touch the keys while he worked the bellows for me. His voice had been so gentle, so patient, and so happy as his hands had guided mine.

I'd felt so secure then. So happy.

By the time *The Sleeping Beauty* actually began, I realized that I wasn't frightened anymore. Dad's silly tune had worked for me, just as the coach's jingle worked for her when she was nervous.

More amazing, I knew what to do! With a kick, I started forward on my right foot. The wall seemed to leap toward me as I built up speed.

I swung my right leg behind me, firmly planted

my pick, drew my feet together, and pressed up into the
air, wrapping my arms around my body as tight
as bandages around a mummy.

For one moment, I felt as if someone had repealed
the law of gravity so that I could just go on floating
through the air forever. But then I was falling again.
Funny, but that little bit of fear was good. It made the
adrenaline race through me. And when I landed on the
sliver of sharp steel, I felt as true and balanced as a ship
floating over a calm lake.

And the best part of it all: it was silent except for
the music. Nobody had laughed.

But I didn't let myself think about that too long.
There was too much to remember, to think, to do.
Everything was happening so fast. I not only had to
perform a particular part of my routine but prepare for
the next step as well. A dozen little things each second:
Hands, feet, posture, balance. It really *was* like trying to
herd butterflies.

And yet I couldn't help smiling from ear to ear
because I loved it. Even if there had been no one in the
rink, I would have wanted to do just what I was doing at
this very moment. And how many people can say *that?*

The world began to whirl around me as I squatted
into a sit spin, head up proudly. Once, twice, on and on,

until I counted six, and I rose, dizzy but my body moving on, just as I'd practiced so many times. There was even some clapping from other parts of the rink besides where I knew my family sat.

They were the longest two minutes of my life, and the best two minutes, too.

And then I was back in the center of the ice, arms stretched up into my final pose, and sad that it was over.

14

Fright Night

I was panting but relieved as I skated off the ice, hardly hearing the applause. I'd done my best—and I'd done my part for the coach. Vanessa's father couldn't use my performance as ammunition against her.

Mrs. Sorokowski gave me a hug as soon as I was behind the curtain, and Anya gave me an even bigger one before she draped my sweater over me.

Then I was too busy to think about anything except helping Mrs. Sorokowski and Anya. Finally, though, we got to the last routine, which was Chad's. He made you feel the music as he skated and yet he leapt and raced around the rink with power.

And then the show was finished. Tired and sweaty, but feeling happier than ever, Anya and I made plans to watch the national skating competition on television in a couple of weeks.

Finally, I made my way into the stands to my family. Along the way, people congratulated me, and when I got to my parents, they looked even prouder than I felt. And rather than making wisecracks, my brothers actually seemed surprised.

"You were great, Sis . . . what happened to you?" Rick scratched his head in frustration as he tried to find the right words. "I mean, it was like you weren't *you*."

"Just stop. The more you talk, the further you shove your foot into your mouth," Skip counseled him.

I smiled at Rick. "It's okay. I found it hard to believe it was me, too."

Perry put his hand almost shyly on my shoulder. "I can see why you chose figure skating." And I could feel the approval radiate from him like heat from a stove.

Someone patted me on the back. I turned to see that it was Nelda, from Nelda's Notions, nodding her head up and down. Her white hair cut into the shape of a helmet always surprises me. "I've seen a lot of skaters in my time, and that wasn't bad for someone your age," she said.

"Didn't I tell you, Nelda?" Bob asked. His wife Mona was there, too, and she reached out to hug me.

"That's our girl," Mona said happily.

"You're not *the* Nelda," Rick said, "the one who owns the sewing stores? With Zuzu the Squirrel?"

"Guilty as charged." Nelda grinned.

I was starting to thank Nelda when I saw some *Temporarily Out of Order* signs in Mona's hands.

Thinking there was some emergency, I asked, "Do you need some help?"

"Naw," Mona said, grinning from ear to ear. "I put this on the snack bar while you were skating."

"And the others went on the restroom doors," Bob added.

"I hope it wasn't too . . . awkward for people," I said, with a grin.

"I took them right off when you were finished," Mona said.

"How was the ice over in the north corner?" Bob asked. "I noticed it seemed a little slow when Anya was out there, so I worked on it when I went out after Vanessa's bead fiasco."

"Perfect, Bob," I said, "thanks." I turned to Mona and my family. "Thank you all." And then I saw the coach coming down the steps toward us. "And thank you," I called up to her.

Coach Schubert nodded with a smile, but I could tell that her mind was already racing ahead into the future. "I'll give you my notes at our next lesson, but what were you doing at the very beginning?" She held her hand over her head and began to wriggle her fingertips.

Dad already knew. "Why, she was playing the

accordion, of course."

The coach laughed. "So you're going to strap on one of them and play as you skate? You'll never land your jumps at Regionals."

"Regionals?" I gasped, right along with my family. Skaters from a certain area compete at Regionals, and only the best go on to Sectionals. From there, the top skaters go on to Nationals.

The coach held up a hand. "You'll go into a non-qualifying event, which means that even if you're on the podium, you won't go on to Sectionals. But it will be a chance to get some experience."

I stared up at her. "You're pushing me again, aren't you?"

"It's my job," the coach said and added, "and my pleasure."

"Pleasure?" I complained. "I just got over being scared, and now you've made me even more frightened than before."

"You're welcome," she said, and then she was busy shaking hands with some other members of the club.

Mom was beaming with pride, while all Dad could say was, "Well, well," over and over.

"Regionals," I said, stunned. Suddenly my legs

turned to jelly, and I would have sat down right on the steps if Perry hadn't caught me.

"Yeah, Regionals," he said, and he and Skip hoisted me up so that I was on their shoulders, as if I had just made the game-winning goal.

"Regionals!" they cheered.

The coach broke off her conversation to shout at them, "For heaven's sake, whatever you do, don't drop her!"

Mom slipped in among my brothers to give me more support. "To Regionals! But first, to Angelo's—to celebrate over pizza," she said.

I felt giddy and scared as my brothers carried me triumphantly toward our car.

What had I gotten myself into now?

Real Girls, Real Letters

American Girl receives hundreds of letters a week from girls asking for help. Here are some real letters from real girls who are learning to develop their talents and to compete in healthy ways.

Unhealthy Competition

Dear American Girl,
I am a figure skater and there's someone who's better than I am. I want to be as good as she is. Every time I have a test, she distracts me. Sometimes I cry. What should I do?
—Frustrated Figure Skater

There will always be people who have more talent than you and others who have less. What matters is that you are doing your best and enjoying yourself. If you think this girl is intentionally trying to distract you, and ignoring her isn't working, talk to your coach. Trying to bring some-one else down is not being a good competitor; it's being a bad sport and an even worse teammate. In the end, though, your best strategy is to stop comparing yourself to this girl (or anyone else). Instead, set goals and work to be the best skater YOU can be.

```
To: American Girl
From: Kicking, but not scoring
Subject: No recognition
```

Dear AG,
My mom is my soccer coach. I like her being my coach, but she never congratulates me when I do something good, like making a save or scoring a goal. How do I ask her to not just point out my mistakes but to recognize my accomplishments, too? Help!

Your mom may be trying hard not to play favorites, but it sounds as if she might be overdoing it, and you miss her support. Start by finding some quiet time away from the soccer field to talk with her. Tell her what's good about having her as your coach, but also explain that you miss her encouragement and positive comments. Chances are she has no idea how you've been feeling. Together you and your mom can find ways to support each other, on the field and off.

Finding Your Talent

Dear American Girl,
My problem is that everyone has a talent but me. I don't have a clue what my talent is. How can I find my talent?
—Talented Out

Finding your special talents can take time and experimentation. Start by paying attention to what you enjoy most. Ask yourself some questions, such as "When am I happiest? Indoors or out?" Do you like to be alone or do you prefer being part of a group? Do you prefer sports or the arts? Then look around your community. What is offered that you might be able to try? The important thing is to pick something that interests you and then give it your best effort. Sometimes trying one thing will lead you to something else, and you'll find your talents along the way. Good luck!

Team Building

Dear AG,
I am a pitcher in softball and I'm really good at it. But when my team thinks I'm going to win the game for them, I get nervous and mess up big-time—right when they need me the most!
—Softball Nerves

Try talking to your coach about what you need from the team when the pressure's on. Is it helpful to hear encouraging comments, or is it distracting? For example, if you make an error or something goes wrong, team members can make a "poof" gesture with their hands to signify, "It's okay, the mistake is gone." This could help you move on and refocus. If you truly feel the support of your team, and if you're all working together, then they'll know and trust that you're doing your best, which should take some of the pressure off. And remember, softball is a *team* sport, and it takes the whole team—not just you—to be successful.

Nerves

Dear American Girl,
I am an ice skater and play the flute. I love doing both, but I have a problem. Whenever I have a test, competition, or solo, I totally freak out. No matter what I do, I get so nervous, I nearly make myself sick, even though I know I can do it. Do you have any tips to help me relax?
—Too Nervous

It sounds as if your nerves are taking the fun out of your performances. Here's a tip to help turn that nervous energy into positive energy: When you start to feel nervous, do some stretches to help your muscles relax. Then take slow, deep breaths, in through your nose and out through your mouth. Shake your jitters out and repeat to yourself, "I'm ready, and I can do this" over and over. Then, when it's "go" time, clear your mind of distractions and focus on the here and now. Trust yourself, and do what you've been trained to do—go for it!

To: American Girl
From: Emily
Subject: Too old?

Dear American Girl,
I am 13 years old, and I've recently started figure skating. Not to be vain or anything, but I'm pretty good. I taught myself spins, jumps, backward skating, and skating on one leg. I'm getting lessons soon, but although people agree that I could do really well, they think I'm "too old" to pick it up and do well in competitions. Now I'm half determined to prove them wrong but also half concerned that I'm just wasting my time. I love skating, but now I'm not sure if it's worth it. What should I do?

If you love skating, do it. And if you dream of skating competitively, lessons from a good coach will help determine if you have the skills, talent, and drive to do well in competition. The ability to compete and to do your very best under pressure can be almost as important as knowing how to do a perfect double lutz. Go for it, and give it all you've got. Even if you don't end up skating competitively, pursuing something you love is *never* a waste of time.

Meet the Author

Laurence Yep has published more than sixty books, and recently he won the Laura Ingalls Wilder medal for his contribution to children's literature. He has been a fan of figure skating since childhood, when he went to see mummies in a museum connected to a skating rink. He wound up watching the figure skaters instead. He is very proud of his official Kristi Yamaguchi bobblehead doll.